T0207864

Books by R. J. Cole

The Dragon's Treasure: A Dreamer's Guide to Inner Discovery (nonfiction)

The Archipelago of Dreams: The Island of the Dream Healer (fiction)

Morpheus Speaks: The Encyclopedia of Dream Interpreting (nonfiction)

Psyche's Dream: A Dragon's Tale (fiction)

PSYCHE'S DREAM

A Dragon's Tale

R. J. COLE

PSYCHE'S DREAM
A DRAGON'S TALE

iUniverse books may be ordered through booksellers or by contacting:

iUniverse
1663 Liberty Drive
Bloomington, IN 47403
www.iuniverse.com
844-349-9409

ISBN: 978-1-6632-1493-5 (sc)
ISBN: 978-1-6632-2727-0 (hc)
ISBN: 978-1-6632-1494-2 (e)

Library of Congress Control Number: 2021917019

Print information available on the last page.

iUniverse rev. date: 08/25/2021

CONTENTS

INTRODUCTION

A Brief Orientation to
Magic as the Masterwork of Psyche's Alchemy

On the ground there is a Hill,
Also, a serpent within a Well:
His Tayle is long with Wings wide,
Already to fly on every side,
Repair the Well round about,
That the Serpent pas not out;
For if that he be there agone,
Thou loosest the virtue of the Stone,
What is the Ground thou mayest know here
And also, the Well that is so cleere:
And else the Serpent with his Tayle,
Or else the work shall little avail …

—George Ripley, alchemist

What foolishness is this? Everyone knows that there's no such thing as magic. You believe there's no such thing, don't you?

Are you sure?

What if I were to tell you that yes, indeed, there is such a thing as magic?

Yes, I know that you've been taught that magic is evil or, at best, fantasy with no intrinsic spiritual value or the rational logic of a science, but the reality is that magic is both good and evil but also neither; highly spiritual; rational, but in a nonrational way; a prescientific activity, yes, but very, very real.

Most psychologists and social anthropologists consider magic, when they consider it at all, as being delusional on behalf of its adherents. But over time the meaning of the word "magic" has degenerated and been demeaned as mere superstition.

At one time in humankind's early history, people's lives were steeped in the magic of the world, and its warm embrace was what kept the people of tribes and villages safe, healed from sickness, and fed. The gods and goddesses of their world provided them with everything they needed, including entertainment and an ace in the hole against their enemies. The modern world has science, which is rational and useful but is often presented as cold, calculating, and often soulless, and it is hard to invoke when the wolf has you backed into a corner.

But the kind of magic revealed here is not of that early form or through modern science, though it certainly existed and is and was practiced alongside both forms.

I first became aware of this magic in the late seventies while walking through a forest in the Santa Cruz Mountains and again was introduced to it over many years by many modern-day wizards of the psyche whom I "chanced" to meet as I grew in my professional practice of psychology.

It was during this first encounter that I became aware of the magic around me. It was as though someone had opened a heretofore unseen door that led me into a numinous forest that took on a faint glow and deep sound that resonated in every cell of my body and grew in intensity as I walked down a mountain trail. And no, I wasn't on any drug other than having come off an hours-long meditation, which can present one with the feeling of being stoned.

I sensed the glow and sound more than I saw or heard them, but they were still very real. The feelings invoked reminded me of the joyful awe I once felt as a child when confronted with something new and powerful. This was a feeling that I had lost touch with along the way to being transformed into a grown-up. It was the magic of the child that I used to be and still am, and when in this space I remembered who I was and was once again drawn to explore anything and everything for no other reason than it is there to be discovered and explored.

It was a place where everything was new, as though it were all happening for the first time. It's a place that I have never fully left, because as with all who have entered this world, the world one is born in becomes a little alien. You can live in this world, but after having seen the other you are no longer of this world.

Real magic cannot be wielded through everyday means and is very difficult to experience if one is stuck on the idea of being a grown-up. Those who still honor the child within and in the affairs of others will find it much easier to pass through the door and find the magic and enchantment that lies beyond. It's when we let go of our same-old, same-old way of being and drop into the chaos of uncontrolled play that the magical child returns.

I think we all long for that place of never-ending imagination where everything is possible through the unfettered expression of the soul that came with us at our birth and where we are the true hero of our own story.

This story is an allegory, partially lived and partially fantastical, that points to an unseen reality. It is a process for entering a reality that cannot be taught but that can show one a "door of perception" that leads into the psychical and unexplainable realm of the magical—the door into that part of our mystical self that holds the often-contrary energies of the universe. It is a story about how we can clean away the visual and mindful impediments that prevent the perception of magic. As William Blake stated, "If the doors of perception were cleansed everything would appear to man as it is, infinite."

This is the magic of the prophets, wizards, angels, and spirits of the deeper world (i.e., our deeper selves), a world that very few have ever seen, and it is not one I can take you directly to or even tell you what it looks like, because each path is individual and must be walked alone. I can act as a guide and talk about the process of what I call walking the ridge to magic, but you will have to find your own way, because my way will not be your way.

Note also that if you read this looking for confirmation of what you think you already know about how reality or magic works, you will be most disappointed. Even the words used to describe magic and reality in this book may not agree with your definitions, for you see, the experiences of which I write are peculiar to me, just as your experience of magic will be to you. But if you will suspend defense of your definitions of individual words and concepts and read the story as a description of the whole instead of its parts, you might get some insight into the magic being referred to.

This story is a tale of the dragons hidden in the caves of the human psyche that are not to be slain but welcomed back to the kingdom that is within each of us. It is a tale of death, reconciliation, and redemption that leads to the reclaiming of magic in the works of humankind.

It is also a story of a young man's coming of age, his discovery of his true nature and calling by taking on an ancient series of seemingly dangerous and impossible alchemical events like those undertaken by the mythological Greek heroes, and his discovery that the greatest treasure of a person does not exist outside himself or herself but within.

These labors of the human psyche include a set of twelve ancient laws that lead this young man into the real magic of life.

It is in this quest that he gains the self-knowledge needed to transmute his ego-self into the sacred-self alluded to in the ancient *Opus Alchymicum*. The process he goes through to become fully aware of his whole ego-self from his psyche's conscious and unconscious mind to the soul, cleanse himself of old ways, and to then open to a new way of being is roughly the alchemical process he needs to go through in order to wield the magic that is all around him.

Mystic journeys such this are fraught with danger and should never be taken lightly or embarked upon without a guide trained in their esoterica.

Like the ancient Greek heroes' journeys, all the metaphorical tasks presented within these pages are about transcending one's illusions and becoming more in touch with the reality that runs all around and through one's life. This is the way to let go of the false-self and open to the spirit, the true self. You and I are a trinity within ourselves—a body, soul, and spirit—with the body being but a garment for the spirit, and the soul its animating force.

The way to this true self, this sacred trinity, is nothing less than a liberation from a faulty and conditioned mindset. I am talking about transcending the stubborn illusions of the world. It's deceptively simple but devilishly hard to accomplish and requires the stamina and heart of a hero or heroine to achieve.

However, the spirit of the door through which we can enter the way is hard to find and often comes to us unbidden no matter how much or how little we have looked. It can come to us in the middle of a dream or while walking down a street we have walked down many times in the past. Sometimes we find ourselves standing before it as if led by some magical spell.

Read now the story of one such person who had been living an ordinary life on an ordinary street, led by the ordinary magic that is life and spirit, who found himself standing before an ordinary-looking door that was unlike any other he had ever seen. Unknown to him at the time, it was the door to the spirit of his true and ordinary self. But what he found behind this door was anything but ordinary. His extraordinary experience recast his consciousness into something totally new.

It is a story of time transcended when an older spirit mentors his younger self and in so doing transmutes the substance of his life.

As for myself, I am still wrestling with the lessons presented and still consider myself a neophyte, though I am somewhat further down the path I stepped out onto when I first walked through that door so many years ago.

Lastly, before I let you pass through the door, I present you with this challenge: listen well, for embedded within the words and the story told lies the secret to what magic is. Can you find it? But once it is found, you will be confronted with an even bigger mystery, because what the secret reveals is the very essence of what is truly magical about reality. As a hint, you will not want to go looking for it or think it into being, for those visions are of the locally conditioned mind and will bind you up. Wait for it in your dreams; moments of solitary reverie and meditation; and that still, quiet place within, and it will find you.

"Dreams is very mystical things," the BFG said. "Human beans is not understanding them at all. Not even their brainiest professors is understanding them."

—Roald Dahl, from *The BFG*

Hand-drawn copy of the fifteenth-century alchemist George Ripley's scroll depicting the transmutation of the dull and leaden human psyche into the golden radiance of its real self.

CHAPTER 1

A New Beginning: Unio Mentalis— The Knowing of Oneself

The world is too much with us; late and soon,
Getting and spending, we lay waste our powers;
Little we see in Nature that is ours;
We have given our hearts away, a sordid boon!
This Sea that bares her bosom to the moon;
The winds that will be howling at all hours,
And are up-gathered now like sleeping flowers;
For this, for everything, we are out of tune;
It moves us not. Great God! I'd rather be
A Pagan suckled in a creed outworn;
So, might I, standing on this pleasant lea,
Have glimpses that would make me less forlorn;
Have sight of Proteus rising from the sea;
Or hear old Triton blow his wreathed horn.

—William Wordsworth

While sitting ever so comfortably before the fire one cold and foggy late afternoon, an old man drew deeply upon his well-used pipe while thinking what it was he wanted to do next in a day that had had no agenda. It was then that he heard a gentle rapping—a hesitant tapping at his living room door.

"What now?" he mumbled aloud as he put down his pipe and rose to answer. This intrusion had caught him by surprise, for it had been some time since anyone had come to visit. Usually, the house would give him a heads-up when a visitor was approaching. But in its defense, it had been so long since the last one it was probably out of practice.

"You are getting sloppy in your old age. You had better shape up!" said the old man to no one in particular, and the house seemed to grumble.

Upon opening the heavy, iron-strapped door, a young visitor stood upon the landing shaking off the mist he had collected while wandering through the empty streets of the Heights neighborhood. He stood there upon the old man's porch, lost in his confusion as to why he had knocked upon this particular door. Then, seeing that the door before him had been opened, he straightened up and, without any greeting or explanation, blurted out, "Can you teach me magic?" *What on earth made me say that?* wondered the boy as he stood there before the old man and looking a little frightened, though with an air of hope. His clothes were all wet, and water dripped from the brim of his hat—one of those straight-billed baseball caps that the old man so hated.

The visitor did not present a good first impression, so the old wizard thought. But as so often before, the spirit had again brought another hopeful to his door. It was not as though he was really surprised by the boy's presence, because as with the others, he had seen him in his dreams. He was, after all, a Wizard of the Veil, a caul-bearer, a man of many minds.

Inwardly he moaned, but he outwardly exclaimed, "No, I cannot!" This was delivered rather brusquely, and he was ready to close the door in the boy's face. But he hesitated, not really expecting this to end this young visitor's quest. He was more interested in the boy's resolve, because it was this resolve that would speak to his level of intention and commitment to his quest. If he wavered now, then he would not be able to make magic anyway, but if he persisted, well then, maybe.

But so many had quit before the real training had even begun. Could he make his intention manifest in the world of illusion, or was he just like all the rest and bound to the world of appearances? It was no use wasting precious time on yet another uncommitted wannabe, and besides, the last thing he needed was a new acolyte underfoot.

"But I want to know. You see, I've forgotten how," he said with a far-off look in his eye.

Now this *is a hopeful sign*, thought the wizard.

"To say you have forgotten how presupposes that you once knew. What say you about that?" he asked as he cocked his head to one side and gestured with his palms outward so as to elicit a response.

"I know that I knew at one time, sometime before this." Again, the boy spoke with a wistful air.

"Have you been here before?"

"My dreams say I have." He looked up at the old man hopefully, sensing that he was showing interest.

"Do they now?" grumbled the old man with much disdain. "What do they tell you about magic?"

"That I need to learn again how to do it," he cried haltingly.

"Well, they are wrong!" Exclaimed the magus with a dismissive wave of his hand. "Magic cannot be learned!" He placed an emphasis on the last word and punctuated his speech by shoving his fists onto both sides of his waist as a gesture of defiance. "What is true is that you are as magic as you will to be." The wizard turned abruptly as if to walk away and exclaimed, "Shut the door before you leave!"

"Please?" cried the young man, looking as if he wanted to get down on his knees and beg.

The wizard knew that to work with this young man would as always have profound effects and changes upon his own person, for every interaction of this nature changed both teacher and neophyte in unpredictable ways. It had been thus with all the young people who had come before, so he was not going to take on another lightly. Even he, in all his accumulated wisdom, did not know the form the changes would take. But this was the path he had chosen, and he could not foresee where it would take him.

Deciding that at the very least this distraction might prove a little interesting and provide some company, even if for a short time, the old wizard turned back and resignedly invited him to exit the dampness and enter. Closing the door gently behind him, he asked, "Do you even know what magic is?"

The boy paused for a moment in thought and then said, "I know that it's everywhere."

Hmm, this boy might have potential. He is open and vulnerable and tells the truth of himself, thought the old man. *He reminds me of my own son, Pan, and is so like the boy I used to be.*

"What do they call you, boy?"

"Uh, my name is Adam."

"Okay, Adam, we will work on it," he offered as he placed his hand on the boy's shoulder, indicating that he wished him to sit on the chair that appeared behind him. As he sat down, he noticed that he was in a large, darkened room with high ceilings and a huge fireplace taking up easily a third of the outside wall, in which a fire was merrily crackling. Candles and several candelabras were scattered about the room, adding their welcoming glow.

Two tufted wing-backed chairs sat near each other, facing the fire, and an old side table sat between them. On this table was a large coffee cup, an unruly stack of papers, a pipe and pipe tray, and a dark green leather-bound book with raised gold lettering on its front. A Celtic triquetra symbol was emblazoned on the cover, and under it were the words "*Tabula Smaragdina.*" This, of course, meant nothing to the boy. Not yet anyway.

Stacks of papers and books of many sizes—some looking very old, with others relatively new—were strewn chaotically about the room, covering just about every horizontal surface. At first Adam wondered why the old guy didn't stack the books on the bookshelves scattered about the perimeter of the room, but when he looked closer, he found that all the shelves were full of books; they were even stuffed in the spaces above books. Clearly this man never got rid of a book; nor did he stop getting them just because he had no more room for them.

Scattered among the books on the tables and stacks on the floor—and, in some cases, hanging from walls or stuffed into bookcase nooks—were several odd-looking artifacts, figurines, ritual masks, and votive offerings that seemed ancient yet in pristine condition as if they were not as old as they looked. Just beyond the room they were sitting in was a veritable cabinet of curiosities and wonders of civilizations and their peoples and their ritual magic. Clearly the old wizard had been collecting these relics for quite some time.

The old man pulled up the other chair and sat down facing the boy. The young man's dark brown eyes widened in anticipation of what may be the most transformative moment of his life.

The old man before him showed questionable fashion sense, what with being dressed in a denim shirt with old, faded jeans and a pair of sandals covering red-heeled purple-polka-dotted socks with a hole where his right big toe was poking through. His long pepper-and-salt hair was tied back with a green ribbon securing a ponytail. He sported a goatee upon his chin with a mustache attached, yet the rest of his face was clean shaven. His eyes were an intense blue gray that, when focused on you, would make you believe he could see into your soul and read your every thought. Adam was to find this very disconcerting at times.

All in all, he was not a bad-looking fellow as far as these magus types go. He looked every bit like one of Adam's professors at the university, though he had never seen this man anywhere around the campus before showing up at his door.

As the old wizard sat, he brushed his hand across the green book and placed his hand upon it as though gaining authority from it. A sparkle of what looked like glitter dust rose from the book and scattered across the table and into the air. He then leaned forward and began to talk. "First of all, young man, you are not normal. You are an anomaly, or you would not be here."

Adam chuckled. "No surprise there. I always thought there was something different about me. Though it usually takes the form of something wrong or broken."

"You are more unbroken than you think and more in touch with your intuitive side than most or you would not have followed the spirit to my door."

"The spirit?"

"It is part of the vital force that animates you and brought you to me. We will talk more about that later, but for now let us focus on your request to learn magic. Your first teaching is that magic cannot be taught. You cannot learn it; it is not a rational thing that can be understood in the conventional way things can be understood, for, you see, it is not a thing. Magic is a field of being. It can be understood, but only in a way that you cannot comprehend. Do you understand?"

The boy looked crestfallen—almost in shock. "N-no," he stammered, looking very much confused.

"Good, that is a start! You will have to learn to let go of your rational mind, that which thinks things through, for you will not find magic through thinking. The rational man does not need magic; therefore, he can never hope to wield it."

"That sounds crazy!" exclaimed the boy disgustedly.

"Precisely!" he said, making his delivery with a long emphasis on the central syllable. "We humans spend so much time thinking about things through the rational brain that we have lost the ability to be magic. Magic cannot be realized in the well-adjusted life where one has learned to accept the so-called rational world and in those who have adjusted themselves to the world of separation, prejudice, survival, avarice, and poverty. One must learn to become, well, maladjusted to the illusions one has been taught to accept. To be and wield magic, one must be able to spot the fantasies of the mind, such as the delusions and illusions and lies that we tell ourselves. The so-called well-adjusted cannot find and wield magic because they believe their fantasies to be real. You have also adjusted to the idea of 'seeing' the world, but have you ever felt it?"

"Of course, I've felt it! I feel its softness, its hardness, its happiness, its sadness."

"And what of it do you not let yourself feel? Until you can feel it all, you are not complete; you are not at peace with yourself. When not at peace, you cannot access or wield magic."

"I don't know what you mean."

"The souls and psyches of all human beings suffer multiple traumas throughout the lives of the bodies that disconnect them from their sources, that archetypal—no, cellular—level of existence between spirit and matter, where magic itself is created and felt on a whole other level than what you have been taught.

"This magic or energy that has been disconnected lies deep within the heart, core self, and immortal spirit. It requires an esoteric discipline reflecting aspects of the mystical and cosmic wonder of the psyche, or totality of the mind, including all its personal and collective elements. When the mind is freed to be what it is, demons and all, it will then allow you to see the magic embedded in everything. It's the place where the dreams of your conscious and unconscious selves meet and share what is real.

"This dissolution from self and spirit requires another dissolution to get back to the original connected body before its birth. When born, the whole fragments and flies off into many unpredictable directions, looking like chaos, yet each piece of the original has a map, or imprint, of the whole. We will be dissolving what separates you from this whole and recombining these pieces to their original state."

The old man paused here to give time for his words to sink in. Of course, at this point Adam had no inkling of what the magus meant by dissolution and recombining, and it was just as well he didn't, or he might have had second thoughts or gone screaming out into the night.

The magus continued his briefing. "The whole and complete human being that leads to magic cannot be attained through division and polarization but through inclusion and acceptance of differences only. Most people live disconnected from their real selves, and it is this that makes them neurotic and unable to access magic."

"But isn't it this separateness, this division, that actually gives rise to purpose and points to the direction one needs to go in in order to become whole?" queried Adam, thinking that he had caught the old guy in an error.

"That is a good point, and to that end the illusion of separateness can play an important role in our self-development. It is important to note that the separation actually makes room for creativity. It is, however, a problem when a person gets stuck in the illusion and it becomes a barrier to wholeness and thus the access to magic. You must be able to move in and out of the illusion when necessary."

"You spoke of dissolution of the self; is this like separation?"

"It is! To heal the rift between humans and the reality they live within, one needs to be able to touch the self—that is, the spirit: the real self. But most people would sooner believe the lie of the illusion than give up their separateness—what they call their individuality—even momentarily. For them separateness is what they also laughingly call their independence. I say 'laughingly' because these people are anything but independent. They are totally run by their unconscious, and what little material they are conscious of has been badly compromised by their conditioned minds. For most of humanity, there is no freedom of choice, no real independence, and thus no chance at wielding magic.

"There are many who have eyes but cannot see, ears but cannot hear, whose hearts are only for the pumping of blood and whose minds recall nothing remarkable. These are the nonmagical people. Those who have found magic live life as a poem with a rhythm and tone alien to most of humanity. This process of opening to magic is transformational and will change your life forever."

This was pretty much a description of Adam's life up until now in that it had been mostly about disappointment, loss, betrayal, survival, and not much room for poetry.

Adam squirmed a little in his seat, already regretting asking for help to learn magic, and this man was going on and on about how he couldn't teach it. *What kind of magic is that? How am I to learn it if this guy can't teach it?*

As though reading the boy's mind, the wizard continued. "Now, I am not referring to the kind of magic practiced by some magico-religious vainglorious nutcase who believes that rituals and thoughts and pleadings for intercession can bring about real-world effects, where ideal causes are mistaken for real ones."

"Not too judgmental, are we?" said Adam sarcastically.

The wizard threw a mock sneer at Adam but went on. "Though having said that rituals are not without value regarding magic in that all rituals were originally designed to aid one in connecting with the divine, which is a prerequisite for practicing magic, all too often people forget a ritual's purpose and adhere to a rigid practice that involves only the inflexible use of certain words and motions. They are also all too often used to manipulate others.

"Rituals are an extension of prayer and, when done with understanding and intention, have positive value and provide a deeper meaning of and connection with the spirit than the empty ceremonies produced by many religionists, cults, or social clubs.

"Nor am I talking about the pointing of some stick and chanting a series of Latin-sounding words to manipulate another person or object or to invoke some deity. That is just fantasy—entertaining, yes, but unreal. That is just sloppy thinking or just *more* thinking and therefore comes through that place in the mind that filters all material on a self-interest level. Magic does not come through the thinking mind and is never about one's self-interest. It could care less about *your* self-interest. Do you get that?" He punched the air in the boy's direction with his index finger for emphasis.

Adam flinched and sat back a little in the chair, quite literally taken aback by the old man's intensity. As time went on, he was to experience this level of intention coming from the old wizard again and again. It was because the old man had no time for the self-centered. He had learned long ago that the meaning of life, and thus its magic, came from the giving of oneself, not the getting, the sacrificing for the greater self and not for the interest and comfort of the smaller self. He had lost too many young people to the folly of an incomplete psyche and would just as soon send this wannabe on his way if he could not bridge the gap between self-interest and self-lessness.

"I get it! But thinking is pretty much what I do all the time. It's easy to say, 'Don't think,' but I've not found a good way around that," said Adam, earnestly trying to understand.

"That is you thinking about thinking. We will work on that. Most of the time, our thinking is used to avoid the place of real magic as though it were a contagion that, if confronted, would throw us into utter confusion and chaos."

"Well, I'm confused!" exclaimed the boy accusingly.

"That is good! Now see if you can just sit with your confusion for a while longer without trying to figure out the meaning of what I say or rejecting what is being said either. Can you do that?"

"I-I think I can," he stuttered tentatively but with a look on his face that seemed to suggest that he thought the old man was a bit mad, though in a reasonable sort of way, of course. It was all very confusing.

"Good! You have now opened just a crack in the door into your deeper self, the place where chaos and confusion live—though some might say that it is in your superficial mind that the chaos resides. But that is neither here nor there. It is in this deeper self that magic also lives. This is the metaphorical star that lives within all humankind and shines from the deeper self, the *sol invisibilis* that makes men and women an astrum, or spark of creation, at their hearts."

9

Why does he put down the use of Latin words and then turn around and use them? Adam thought to himself. He then blurted out, "Can you teach me this spark, this hidden light? Is it the magic of which you speak?"

"I cannot teach you the way of magic, but I can introduce you to where it lives and let you discover it and walk with it yourself."

"So, if I learn the way, can I then summon it when I wish?" queried Adam, still stuck on the idea of being able to do magic.

"Magic can never be summoned; it arises at its own will, not yours. The magical is lawless and occurs through chance—though there are laws that increase your chances of ever seeing it. Because it is everywhere, it does not need to be summoned. But you can learn to open to it. The truth is that it comes from disarray."

Seeing no light in the boy's eyes yet, the wizard asked, "Who is responsible for running your life?"

"Well, uh, I am!" he exclaimed as though it were obvious.

"But what if you were to find out that this has never been true?"

"What? Really?" he squeaked. "I mean, I'm the one who decides who controls what, right?"

"Well, the 'you' that you identify as being you never was in control; it is not so even now! The chaos and confusion that you shut off into your unconscious runs you more than that little bit of mental territory you call consciousness. You spend so much time and energy trying to be what you are not that you have hidden what you are. The magic you seek is all around and within. You are the magic but cannot see it!"

For one moment, the light in the young man's eyes shone through the darkness, very briefly, and then it was gone. "What was that?" asked the wizard to get the boy to focus.

"What was what?"

'The look on your face. What just passed through your mind?"

"I–I don't know," he stammered, looking even more confused and feeling very weary and just a little stupid.

"Straighten up and sit there for a moment. Quiet your thoughts and listen to the voice talking in your head, the one that is saying, 'What voice? I do not hear any voice!' Just let it talk without engaging it. Be with the voice. Do it now, and we will talk more later."

Adam sat for a moment and let his thoughts begin to quiet. *Nothing!*

This is a waste of time! cried the voice in his head. *Ahh,* that *voice—that's what he means,* came the voice once again. "But who is it talking to?"

Listening without engaging, he chose to just let the voice be, and after a short while with nothing engaging the voice, there was a moment when all became quiet. He could hear his own breathing and feel the warm air from the fire brush against his cheek and rustle the hairs on his forearms. Then something wordless from deep within "spoke" to him.

There was another presence making itself known—something he had not noticed before. Something else was *with* him … no, *in* him … no, of him. He suddenly opened his eyes and exclaimed in a hushed whisper, "I heard it! What is that? Who is that?"

The old sage chuckled softly and exclaimed almost under his breath, "The journey has begun," and then he brought the conversation to a close by getting up and walking to the door and motioning for the boy to leave. "See you tomorrow, same time."

The young man's face literally beamed. He fairly hummed with a jumbled mix of delight, anticipation, and fear. He then turned and almost skipped from the room, opened the door, and strode out into the night.

The magus picked up his still smoldering pipe and took a long, leisurely draw, slowly exhaling and engulfing himself in smoke.

CHAPTER 2

Detachment as the Gateway to Magic: The Transcendental Expressed through Paradox

Adam awoke late the next day. "Damn!" he muttered. "I've slept through both classes. I'll get notes on the mythology class from Julien later," he told himself, but he knew that he couldn't always trust Julien to go to class either. As this was running through his mind, he realized that he was about to be late for his time with the old magus as well, and he abruptly rolled out of bed to his knees, straightened awkwardly, and hopped to the bathroom, intending to shower. He then changed his mind, given that he was already dressed, what with having fallen asleep on the bed from the exhaustion experienced the day before with the old magician.

As he turned on his heels to head out of the bathroom, he changed his mind once again, pivoted back, grabbed some toothpaste, and squeezed some into his mouth, rubbed his teeth with his right index finger, stretched to get the kinks out of his body, and then trotted toward the kitchen and again changed his mind and doubled back toward his room.

His roommates were gone, so he had the whole place to himself and wouldn't have to explain why he was running around like a crazy man. But then he was always running around like a crazy man, always late, always a little behind.

He grabbed a stick of deodorant and quickly rubbed some under his arms, slipped on his shoes, picked up his jacket from where he had tossed it on the floor earlier, and ran back toward the kitchen. There he scooped up a piece of cold pizza sitting in an open box that one of his mates had left on the counter and pulled open the fridge, looking for what was left of the milk, but found only an empty carton. "Darn! Why do they put an empty carton back in the fridge?" he mumbled aloud, but he then headed for the door, tossing the offending carton into an already full trash can, where it bounced out and onto the floor to collect with the rest of the tossed refuse from the neglected bin. He then skipped over a set of barbells lying on the floor while trying to stuff the limp pizza wedge into his mouth, but in his rush, he nearly broke his toe at the edge of the sofa.

"Why does this always happen?" he yelled. Hopping on the other foot and grumbling with the pain, he stood up straight and bolted out the door, barely taking time to lock it behind him, and charged down the stairs and into the street. It was then that he let out a big sigh.

It was late afternoon, and the rows of aging Victorian houses two and three stories high with their elaborately architectural, ornamented, and multicolored façades had taken on a glow of warmth as though readying themselves for the end of another day.

Stepping out into and glancing down the street, he could just see the corner bodega and wondered if he had time to grab a quart of milk but decided that he didn't. As he turned back to the curb, a bicyclist flying down the street barely missed him. "Damn fool!" each grumbled at the other as he flew past.

Though the sky was still light, the large picture frame windows of some houses shone with a warm amber glow that added to the sense of their aliveness. He had always loved this time of the day; even as a kid, he would wander out and wonder what the families inside the other houses were doing. He would imagine all the great things that were missing in his empty home and would envision them into the houses with the glowing windows. Though he didn't know these people, it helped him to feel less alone.

As the young man skittered up the tree-lined street, he couldn't remember the last time he'd been this excited about something—about anything. Not since he'd lost his last foster family to a drunk driver had he the energy to do much of anything in earnest.

He almost flew over the sidewalk, grabbing a rowan tree sentry with one hand at his destination, which almost seemed to push him forward, and used the momentum of his run to swing him around and onto the walkway leading up to the three-story house where his new mentor lived.

Adam looked back at the tree and thanked it for its assistance. The tree seemed to shake its leaves in response.

"Oh God, what if I'm too early or too late? He didn't say what time I should show up except that it should be about the same time as yesterday. I don't want to make him angry before we really get started. Magic … imagine, me, learning to do real magic," he mused aloud as he slowed his pace while walking across the long entrance to the staircase at the other end, where he paused to gather his wits.

"What was it he said? 'You can't "learn" magic.' And then he droned on endlessly. 'Learning is through the thinking mind,' he exclaimed, and he told me the process of discovering that I already know the magic is something that he could help me with, though I'm not sure about what the old man meant by the 'already know' part. I mean, what *do* I know?" he wondered aloud.

He stopped at the foot of the stairs, unsure as to whether he should go up. After all, he had been so confused the night before. What made him think that this evening would be any different?

Summoning his courage, he climbed to the first-floor entry and knocked on the wizard's door. He heard a muffled "Enter" and tried the knob, entering slowly and peering around the door, and then catching a glimpse of someone sitting in a much worn and overstuffed brown leather chair, with pipe smoke curling up and disappearing somewhere into the exposed witchwood rafters above.

The flickering light from a fire in the heavy stone-mantled fireplace lit a small area around the old man's chair, leaving the rest of the cavernous room in darkness.

This time he noticed that the room was warm, musky, and smelled of cherries and old books—a rather inviting fragrance, he thought. Something else caught his eye, and he stared into the fire and swore that he could see small fire creatures dancing across the tops of the flames. As he looked closer, the sound of the wizard broke his trance.

"You are just in time," enthused the old man as he pulled the pipe from his mouth and set it smoldering in the bowl next to him.

Adam let out a breath of air with a big sigh and just then noticed that he had been holding his breath in anticipation.

Without even a "good evening," the old magus motioned the boy to sit on the braided rag rug before him and began to talk. Adam felt a little as though he were back in kindergarten, sitting on a carpet square before the teacher; and now, as then, he was full of fear, excitement, and anticipation for all the wonders to be revealed.

The old man waved his hand through the air, and the room filled with light.

"There, that is better; we can see each other now. First, you need to remember that magic is not about things. Things have no magic, though there are those who use things, like idols, for magical effect. To the degree that your consciousness is preoccupied with things—the having and not having of them, and your unending compulsive plans around your life—to this degree you will not be able to produce any magic.

"I will not teach you magic, but I will teach you how to open the door to it. There is a greater spirit beyond that which is recognized and worshiped in the religions of most of humankind. It is from this truth that magic flows. This is not the magic of medicine bags, wands, idols, incantations, and charms; nor is it the magic of tranquilizers, drugs, rationalism, positive thinking, or the power of your will—at least not the will of your smaller self."

"My smaller self?"

"Yes, yes. You have two selves; the smaller is the one you are most familiar with, and the bigger is your essential self, your real self. We will go into that in much more detail when you have had the experience of this bigger self."

"Sounds intriguing! Can I experience it now?"

"Not if you keep interrupting!" the magus exclaimed. "Now where was I ... oh yes, the things that we collect on our spiritual journey through life are not the source of power; it is their meaning to the person who honors them that is the source of the power. You cannot even begin to see what magic is if you are attached to the world of things. When you realize that you are not one of those things but rather are the container of all things, then and only then will you be open to magic.

"Let me be clear; *things* are a false prophet. Beyond the basics of physical survival, love, and belonging, there is nothing that needs to be attained, or even held on to, that is of any real or lasting value. We are complete and with nothing left out. Anything worth being we already are, there is nothing missing. All the striving is just so much noise. Whether we think of ourselves highly or are burdened by self-criticism and doubt, it is just so much noise."

"But what's wrong with things?" Adam asked.

"Do not mistake my words; there is nothing wrong with things or even in their having. We can have as many things as we want, and the process of getting and having the things can be fun, but the things are not going to make any real difference in our lives. The degree to which we are 'attached' to these things is also the degree to which we cannot experience magic.

"The very act of unconditional giving or detachment magically becomes a receiving, whereas acts of mostly getting create a dissonance that will separate you from the magic. In short, anything that separates will keep you from the magic. Why do people hoard things such as objects, money, food—whatever?"

"Well, I guess to survive a future time when they won't have them."

"Yes, but that suggests that their worldview is one of not enough, limit, and scarcity. But that view only drains the energy for realizing magic, whereas letting go of these attachments allows for the flow of energy that leads to magic.

"What we will be doing from here on is disentangling you from all inner and outer attachments of your life—that is, all the things that you believe are real and necessary to life."

"Uh, excuse me, professor, but with all due respect, you seem to be quite attached to your collection of junk spread out on every surface around here. I mean, there's chaos everywhere!"

"Ah, but there is a symmetry to my chaos; everything is sorted by how high the stacks are."

"That sounds to me like the definition of 'clutter,'" said Adam with a slight grin."

"Never you mind, young man. One man's clutter is another man's filing system. Now where was I?"

"I think you were talking about disentanglement," Adam said with a slight indictment while he moved his hand across the room covered in all the whatnot.

The magus frowned and went on. As he talked, the room seemed to clear itself of all the so-called clutter, leaving all the surfaces free and clear. Adam was about to say something but then thought better of it.

"Right now, you operate as though the only part of your mind that is of real importance is your conscious mind. The conscious mind is that part of you that thinks it knows what is real, but it is like a wall between you and reality. It literally creates the reality that you see, and that reality is often a false experience. Reality is not just one but many. Your mind is caught in only one of those many. By this limitation you are looking through a dark window into your deeper mind—what an old friend of mine called 'a glass darkly.'

"When your idea of self can disentangle from the false identity, the current center of your consciousness, and open to the space between it and the unconscious mind, you will create a new center of being that will then allow you to tap into and include the unconscious, become fully human, and be magic. This is a place of spiritual emptiness—that is, a space of silence where only the real can enter. Spirituality must engage both the conscious and unconscious mind, and magic demands it. Do you understand?"

"I ... I do, sort of, though I ... I'm still confused as to how I get there." The boy stammered as he trembled at the thought of what "there" might mean.

"The first thing you will have to do is to give up your attachment to all things," affirmed the old man rather dryly and without emotion.

"What? What do you mean? Give up my attachment to everything? You mean give up everything I own? Are you kidding?" He noted that this was beginning to sound a lot like all those boring sermons at church when he was a kid. He wasn't any more likely to give up all that he had worked so hard to get now than he had been back then, when he thought it meant giving up his action figures collection and video game console. He didn't think at that time that it was much of a heaven where one couldn't have those things, and the stakes were even higher now.

"I mean, you must give up your attachment to these things, including your ideas about them. You are attached to the outer world, and that is your greatest obstacle to the introspection necessary for discovering your magic. You believe that you need these things in order to survive or be happy, do you not?"

"Most of them, yes ... yes, of course!" The boy exclaimed emphatically.

"Most of them?" queried the old man as he raised one eyebrow.

"Well ... food, water, breathing seem like necessary attachments, don't you think?"

"You are talking about being attached to living and to the avoidance of dying, am I right?"

"Of course! I would think avoiding death at all costs would be an obvious goal," said Adam defensively.

"The many thoughts of death are unique to the human animal. While other animals just instinctively react to any potential death threat, humans think about it a lot prior to and after any actual threat. However, for humans the thoughtful concept of death organizes one's life. It is what brings vitality to one's living when one acknowledges the presence of it at every turn. Life and death is just another polarity where when one resists the struggle it's apparent conflict fractures the whole and limits the expression of the magic. The whole idea of free will depends on the struggle and the embracing of death. Your attachment to its avoidance can limit your full expression. Do you not see this?"

"I do, but if you don't mind, I'd like to stay alive, though I can appreciate the value that this desire can have upon the way I live my life."

"Okay, for now let us move on. You also believe that no rational person would give up everything to go chasing after some fantasy, do you not?"

"I do."

"Do you label your fantasies as just daydreaming—something to just while away some boring hours but without any real substance?"

"Mostly, yeah!" he exclaimed while wondering where the old man was going with this.

"Be careful here, for it is the essence within your fantasies, my dear boy, that enables magic. When it comes to magic, your rational mind is your biggest obstacle to wielding it. The magic lies within the irrational, and by that I do not mean the opposite of rational but a space beyond the rational. To become it, you have to be willing to embrace even death."

This last part of course shocked the boy, and he became highly alert and suspicious of the old man's intentions. He quickly looked about him for some avenue of escape should he need it. The room was dark all around them except for where they were sitting. He wasn't sure where he would go if he had to move quickly. He could feel the fear swell in his chest, and his shoulders began to tighten as though getting ready for action.

Noticing the boy's change of affect to one of fear, he quickly interjected. "Not the death of your body, for goodness' sake! I am talking about detachment from that well-regarded ego-self of yours that dominates your every move and your every thought. The ego does not know magic! It cannot because magic does not come from one's ego. But first one needs to know what makes up this ego—both the conscious and unconscious parts of it and its body—to then transcend it. And by 'transcend' I do not mean to get rid of it. It is the necessary container for the spirit and your spiritual insight while on Earth, but to touch the beyond and thus its magic, one needs to learn how to get outside it.

"The ego-self is all about control. It is part of the defensive self that is only needed if you do not feel safe. The truth is you are not in control anyway. It is the part of you that defines who you are when you do not know who you are.

"The ego is about a singular point of view and is willful in nature. When it decides on its point of view, it rules out all other points of view and leaves you spiritually myopic. Your ego can be your prison. It is what prevents you from fully loving and belonging. The truth is that if you look closely, Adam, it is exhausting not being who and what you are.

"It is what keeps you separated from the magic. Things will work much better when you get your ego-self out of the way; this is what the rituals and chemical inducements of the shaman, the wizard, and the witch are all about, in that they are making room for the soul by getting the body or ego-self out of the way. It is also what prayers of confession are designed to do so that the ego-self is no longer defending itself. Understand?"

"You seem to think that who I think I am is something different than who I really am," The boy protested defensively. "This is me; what you see is what you get—what I really am."

"Really? Are you sure about that? What if I told you that your personality, the thing that you think you are—this ego-self and the personality masks you wear—are not who you really are, but that it is all made up?"

"I'd say you were crazy."

"You said that the last time we met. But can you hold the image of that possibility that you are not what you say you are? Can you just for the next few days sit with the notion that you have no idea who you really are? Can you just sit in that space of vulnerability without being defensive?

"You have many things in your life—objects and ideas, such as your name, your degree, your size, your beliefs, your likes and dislikes, who your parents are, family traditions, cultural traditions, the foods you like and do not like, the style of clothes you wear, the music you like, politics, sports teams, and the type of girl you are interested in—all of which you have attached to your identity. Add to these all your adaptations in behavior to please your parents, teachers, and friends. All these things and more are what you have attached to yourself and then call your personality. What would you be if they were all gone? What would you be if you were to just be unattached to anything?"

"Well, I, I don't know," he exclaimed hesitatingly.

"Go home and detach. Let go of or surrender that darn thing that you call 'you.' Be open to something much bigger than your ego-self. Be without it for a while, and then tell me who you are. This is also the way to magic.

"Do not come back until you do—until you have let go of everything. And by everything, I mean your past, past hurts, past insults, and present judgments of yourself and of others that come out of past decisions, past wins, and losses. Forgive the reality of your past for what it was and what it was not. You are not living in the past; you live only in the present.

"Most people are letting their image and experiences of the past dictate how they see and respond in the present; their consciousness is not in the present. They let earlier and similar events activate what they see and do in the present. No wonder they make so many mistakes; they cannot see what is in front of them, but only what was in front of them at an earlier time. It is no wonder they cannot practice magic; magic only exists in the here and now."

"But how do I let go of the griefs and grievances of the past?" pleaded the young man.

"All the sadness, hurt, anger, and grief of our lives often grows out of a sense of loss. You have no doubt experienced suffering and disenchantment, and it has bowed you. You probably made some decision about how you were never going to suffer like that again and then shut the door to your feelings to honor your pledge. Shutting yourself off from your feelings also shuts you off from magic. How you display courage in your suffering or in the memory of it—that is, how you leave the door open—will affect how you deal with it and then let it go."

"Sometimes it just isn't logical to deal with feelings."

"But feelings are never logical, and you cannot coerce logic to suit your feelings. You also cannot avoid these feelings. You cannot shove them down and not have them. What you must do is have them, stop struggling with them, name them, be with them, and go through them without engaging them. Having the feelings without resisting them is transformative; trying to fix them is not.

"Do not hide from your feelings—neither the ones that you call good nor the ones you call bad. Acknowledge the feelings that may be evil, such as hate, revenge, jealousy, and the like, for these are normal for all of us to some degree.

"Also, call out all your thoughts for what they are, just thoughts, just as feelings are just feelings. It is when you make the thought or feeling real by believing it is true and never ending and start acting it out in how you treat yourself or in how you treat others consciously or unconsciously, intentionally, or unintentionally, that your thoughts and feelings can manifest. Name these thoughts and feelings and let them be, do not run with them."

"What about thoughts of reflecting what you did wrong in the past or those where some wrongs were done to you? Don't you need to hold on to them so that it won't happen again?"

"And for your actions in the past, forgive yourself for what you did or did not do. Know that you could not then have done anything other than what you did when you did it, and that nothing other than what happened could have happened. Use the experiences as lessons for how you are being now."

Bewildered, Adam got up and looked sheepishly at the wizard because he was not sure what he was asking of him, but he resolved to at least try and then absently wandered out of the room, saying a barely audible "goodbye" as he closed the door behind him, started down the stairs, and walked into the night.

Strolling home, he looked out across a cityscape that was here and there covered in fog and landed his gaze upon one of his favorite visions. Peeking through the fog, a lighted bridge with vermillion spires highlighted by flashing red beacons jutted across the darkened deeps of the bay's entrance and seemingly disappeared into the mist before getting to the other side. A wry grin crossed Adam's face when he realized that this was like a metaphor for the way he felt—incomplete and only partially there.

Meanwhile, the magus picked up his still smoldering pipe and took a long, leisurely draw, thereafter, slowly exhaling and engulfing himself. Tiny rings of smoke grew wider as they floated upward and were swallowed by the darkness above.

Feeling a chill, he shivered and drew the fire ever closer. In his mind's eye, the room seemed to flicker, and a canopy of stars spread out across what had once been his parlor ceiling. With another puff of his pipe, he stretched out. "Once again we climb down the rabbit hole," he whispered, as though talking to some unseen entity, leaving only his grin glowing through the smoke.

CHAPTER 3

Beginner's Mind: The Primordial Mind

If one has done ones best to steer the chariot, and one then notices that a greater other is actually steering it, then magical operation takes place.

—C. G. Jung, from *Lieber Novus*

It had been three days since he last left the old wizard. The sky was heavy with rain. Water rushed like a whitewater rapid down the street, filling gutters like a dam's spillway, washing all the flotsam and jetsam from the neighborhoods high on the hill toward the city center below. Here and there the street drains were filled with so much debris that small lakes formed around them, obliterating the intersections, and making it difficult for the cities' traffic.

A wind blew down from the top of the hill with its full force channeled by the rows of houses, with the narrow streets driving the rain deep into any nook or cranny in the well-kept buildings and any person foolish enough to be outside on a day like this.

But a young man braved this storm wearing only a short slicker and a knit cap, hoping to arrive at his destination before being thoroughly soaked. Of course, it was not to be, and soon he found himself standing before the familiar door and waiting for what seemed an eternity, dripping from every fiber of his being, for the invitation to enter. After knocking yet a second time, a gruff voice could just be heard over the din of the rain: "Enter."

He entered and stood in the foyer, creating a small puddle on the floor beneath him, and he smiled self-consciously; shook the water from his hair, brushing it vigorously with his hand; and took off his jacket to hang it on the hook directly across from the door. Before he could squeak out a greeting, the old man began speaking.

"Sooo, did you let go of all your attachments?" asked the old man with a barely disguised hint of doubt and sarcasm in his voice.

"Yes. It wasn't easy, but, yes!" the young man exclaimed as he removed his sodden shoes and nudged them to the side.

"And?"

"And nothing! No magic, no nothing!" the boy declared in anger and disgust as though he had been duped. The perceived failure of the last three days, along with the miserable weather, had ruined his mood, leaving him none too polite with his mentor's incessant questions.

"Then you did not detach." The old man exclaimed with an air of dismissal.

"I did so!" declared the boy stubbornly.

"Did you expect that when you finally detached then you could do magic or feel or be different in some way?"

"Yes, of course!"

"Then you were still attached to the outcome. You probably had the thought that I had ripped you off in some way, and that thought instantly took you over and you could not let go of it. That is another attachment—attachment to your thoughts, which the ancients called the stinking waters of mere mortals. You probably felt proud of yourself for having been so successful with your so-called detachments, did you not?"

"Yes, I did!" he asserted defiantly, nearly spitting out the words.

"More attachment! Pride, thoughts, beliefs, expectations, thinking that you know something. You are imprisoned in a brain that thinks it knows but does not know. Let go of thinking you know; embrace 'not-knowing.' Too much knowing fills you up, leaving no room for anything new. Give up your knowing; then perhaps you will be able to know something. You need to know yourself to access magic, but you do not know yourself. Give up thinking that you do."

"Whew! Does your tongue get stuck in your cheek when you talk about knowing your knowing?"

Ignoring Adam's comment, the magus went on. "As humans, most of what we think we see is subjective in nature and often misses what is objectively there. Yet, and this is a big yet, our subjective experience of something objectifies it. The meaning of anything is a projection of both the outside and the inside of every person. Our expectations for ourselves and others, and those that others have for us, project the subjective experience onto the objective reality and cloud it but also inform it."

"Uh, projections?"

"Yes, the judgments, ideas, and meaning that we all place upon another person, a thing, or an event that are purely subjective and may or may not have any reality. We do it all the time—so much so that we rarely see the true reality of anything. This shows up strongly in our relationships, in that there are expectations within all relationships (emotional or contractual) that each party will behave in a certain way, and one party expects the other to reciprocate. To the degree that we can free ourselves from our subjective projections and expectations, this is the degree to which we can perceive reality. Until then we are not really exercising free choice and therefore cannot be magic."

"You make relationships sound so manipulative!"

"For many people, they are. Often is the case that when we say to the other, 'I love you,' what is it that we expect in return?"

"Well, I guess something like 'I love you too'!"

"Exactly. There is an unwritten contract or expectation that is often a manipulation of the other. Let me repeat expectations are a big no-no in the practice of magic. You must expect nothing because expectations only limit you to what you already think you know or think you need and will prevent you from experiencing real knowledge or discerning real need. It is a form of pride and arrogance, with pride used as a justification for negative action when it is never a justification for anything. And arrogance can cause myopia, a constriction of the reality seen, and sometimes blindness, in which one cannot see what is in front of or around one.

"Arrogance can also make you stupid or make you do stupid things.

There is no limit to the number of stupid lengths some people will go to, and arrogance can lead to haughtiness, contemptuousness of others, and the disdain of all things you do not believe in or think you know.

"Yes, there are also those annoying beliefs—what a farce! Adherence to all your beliefs leads you astray to always think you are right, and you become attached to your righteousness." The old man shook and lowered his head as though trying to rid his mind of an unwanted thought.

"But what if you are right?"

"Okay, what if you are? This desire for rightness is a road to oblivion, while on the other hand, if you accept your mistakes and embrace the imperfections of life, you open yourself to the creative spirit.

"A mind is endarkened by such things as desire, pride, greed, arrogance, self-righteousness, fear, and hate, which are all based on inflexible beliefs and self-centered points of view. All these emotions trap the will, and this makes it nearly impossible to see magic, let alone wield it. A mind thus distracted becomes not only susceptible to more of the same but also open to false magic, where irrational and disconnected wishful thinking leads to a never-ending fall down a rabbit hole of despair and darkness that consumes its light."

"But don't our beliefs ground us and give us a place that's safe to operate from? And what about those beliefs that actually protect us?"

"You mean like placebos? Yes, a belief that something will work often results in that thing working. But its working is usually only on a superficial level, in that it can alter a perception of something like pain but not cure what is causing the pain. The belief or expectation can affect the body's chemical response because there is a cellular link between body and mind.

"These beliefs can also, on occasion, affect the body's immune system, which can affect and protect the body. Concentrated mantras, including prayer, that focus on the body can also provide positive brain–body interaction, as can proper motivation. Those who have become addicted know how hard it is for a brain to overcome the neural changes that come from an addiction, but a shaman knows that with proper and sustained motivation and behavior management, these changes can be mitigated and eventually overcome.

"Ha, even laughter can affect the body and well-being of the mind!

Wizards and shamans have always known of these links. It is why they have been so effective in certain societies over many millennia.

"Knowing the mind's places of being hardwired versus those places that are more malleable and responsive to suggestion or conditioning is also knowledge that has been exploited by these shamans and healers through a ritualistic and therapeutic act. This understanding of the body–mind connection can act as an effective tool in the art of wielding magic."

"This sounds like manipulation. I thought you were against that."

"It is manipulation, but purpose and motivation weigh in here. If used to open the mind to magic, the creation of a ritual designed to do that can be quite useful. But to believe that all these effects are always true is where one gets tripped up. Beliefs are singular points of view that, when embraced, rule out all other points of view and make one spiritually myopic and closed to magic. Beliefs can and do create expectations. When the expectations are not met or are thwarted in some way, it often leads to resentment. Resentment is a poison that keeps you stuck and unhappy and makes it eminently more difficult to move on. Essentially it makes you a prisoner to the situation and circumstances. And when stuck and unable to move on, the door is shut to magic."

"So you might say that we should expect the unexpected."

"It is what we in the magus trade would call a black swan mantra because black swans are always full of surprises. Be open to surprise and you will be open to magic. Every event, every circumstance, and, for that matter, every person is different and therefore subject to surprises.

"In the world of today, we have let our differences and our beliefs about those differences blind us to the spirit that we all share. The three parts of ourselves—body, soul, and spirit—have been separated in our modern world, and it is this separation that needs to be conjoined to permit us to be opened to magic. This separation impairs our ability to actualize the unified self and thus our full access to magic."

"But there are differences, aren't there?"

"Yes, but what would happen if this point of view of focusing on our differences and uniqueness were shifted to one of asking what binds us all together? What would happen if we were not all so interested in our own personalities?"

Who We Are at Our Cores: The Machina Mentis

"In our insistence on maintaining the illusion of being separate individuals, we are not able to see the wholeness of who we are. The truth, Adam, is that we are already whole. In our preferred illusion that everything is separate from everything else, human from human, human from animals or the flora of the forest, or being not of heaven or the earth, we have limited our power. When we are alienated from the reality of our wholeness, ill health can get a foothold.

"All beings possess the potential to access the infinite wisdom of the spirit, and the individual has the ability to know the whole by becoming like the whole. I can tell you the secret of who we are, but it will mean nothing to you until you have become it. We are not the body; it is only a tool to do a certain job while in this level of existence. We are not the body's mind, senses, feelings, pains, griefs and joys, thoughts, desires, scars, or memories; those are just aspects of the tool that the essence of what we are uses to experience and work in the current manifestation of existence."

"I'm having trouble here because, as I see it, I'm over here and you are over there. We are separate. There is always a me and they or an us and them."

"It does appear that way. But, Adam, you are not only a you, but you are also a them. They see you as part of the them, do they not? To others, you are an 'other.' To those you label as bad, you are bad. This is what maintains the illusion. This is what keeps you from seeing what you really are. The story told by all of us is that we are separate. We take as self-evident that there is an I and there is a them. The simple truth is that each person is a part of you that you just do not know yet. But without knowing who and what we are, we become vulnerable to the adversities of life and become bound and restricted by our limited knowledge of self and thus cannot be magic. Without knowing who we are, we have only assumptions."

"What about assumptions?"

"Assume nothing because it can negatively affect the reality perceived. To assume is to have an expectation that something is or will be a certain way, and as I have said, this gets in the way of magic. So, I advocate that you abandon all your assumptions; most of them are probably wrong anyway."

"But what if just about everyone agrees that your assumption is correct?"

"Surly you can see that does not mean that the assumption is correct. And why would agreement be so important? What if everyone does not agree?"

"Then it might be hard to have a rational discussion."

"And there you go again, trying to find the magic in the rational. Agreement in this case is just a reflection of what the people are being and seeing in the moment and their cultural conditioning, and it may have nothing to do with reality. Given that most people see reality through the eyes of fear, ignorance, arrogance, limiting beliefs, and false assumptions, all you would have with mass agreement would be mass error.

"All of these emotions, if left alone, can tether people to a limited way of being from which there can be no experience of magic. But it is magic itself that can make us courageous enough to deal with the limits we place on ourselves. The courage and its commensurate magic is there if people are willing to learn how to tap into it.

"Basically, we do not see reality but only the image of what we have conceptualized it to be. In other words, we form an idea of the reality we experience and then think that our idea or concept is the reality."

"Okay, scratch assumptions. Check."

"These expectations and assumptions of yours actually affect what you see and do not see. Some folks call them cognitive biases. They will determine your reality. They affect your interpretation of reality. I bet that you think you have no role in reality—that there is reality and then there is what you make of it. Not so! You are making it with every observance, interpretation, decision, and action."

"I don't have the experience that I'm creating reality. Things happen, and then I have to deal with them."

"Ask yourself to what degree you create the reality that you see. To what degree do you create the reality of pain and grief and separation? Better yet, to what degree will you take responsibility for it? Most humans are quick to project responsibility—blame, really—for what happens to them onto someone or something else to remain guilt free in their own minds. This approach is both consciously and unconsciously rejecting responsibility, which often is viewed as burden. The witch trials and condemnations of shamans over the centuries and across the globe is evidence of the lengths people have gone to handle their fears and questionable actions and beliefs by laying blame on something outside themselves. In general, people do not want the burden of responsibility for the reality they created and are confronted with. If they cannot lay it onto one another, which is at the core of prejudice, they make a god responsible by suggesting that it is God's will or that our actions have brought on his wrath. One does not have to look far for examples.

"On another level, responsibility is not just for the darker aspects. Are you not responsible for creating a reality of inclusiveness, communion, wholeness, and happiness as well?

"Not to get too complicated with the idea of our interconnectedness but imagine all of us humans as one giant neural network attached to a universe of networks, both physical and temporal, and imagine multiple time streams in parallel creating an even greater network of universes."

"That's way too hard for this brain to wrap itself around. Could you just bring it a little closer to home?"

"Okay, let us use the experience of communion to illustrate the connectedness at our core. At the moment of communion, is not the illusion of the reality of separation banished? And in that moment, what is it that you feel?"

Adam stood silent, trying to recall a time when he felt deeply connected with someone, and he remembered Jenny, beautiful redheaded Jenny, and his heart leaped quickly yet sank almost as fast. Memories came flooding back: the smell of warm cinnamon, a walk along a beach, racing for cable cars in bare feet, the silly act of eating carnations because they smelled like they could be eaten, running red lights to get her back to her parents' house before curfew, and oh, that smile that would light up a room. As always, his heart ached at her memory, and the tears still flowed.

Since her loss, he had just been wandering, lost and lonely, with an emptiness that just couldn't be filled no matter how hard he tried. He looked upward as he had done so many times before when he got in touch with the pain. Looking upward was his way of trying to connect with God—a God he'd never had a direct experience of, but when feeling lost he always tried for contact. After all, who else could he turn to? As always, it would help soothe the hurt but never heal it. He shook his head as though to cast out the feelings and came back into the room where his mentor sat waiting.

"Love!" he declared. This was mostly what he felt. His love for her was as though he had found himself in her and she in him. Even with all the hurt and anger he felt for the loss of family, his love for her was like morphine against the pain. It was as if in those days he could feel nothing else but love. But with that connection there was also profound grief when he lost her, when the connection was broken. Communion and loss always seemed to come hand in hand. It was as though connection and separation lived within each other.

The magus's questions were triggering something in his life that he had always tried to forget, though not very successfully.

"Exactly! Love, the *machina mentis*—what we are essentially at our core," responded the old wizard. "It is what ties everything together and raises everything on high. When only connected to yourself, you are inclined to be responsible only for yourself and family, but when connected to everything, when you see that in essence you are everything, what then?"

Sensing that the magus was waiting for an answer, he blurted, "Then I'm responsible for everything?"

"Yes! But do you really get that?"

"I do, but I'm not sure I want it."

"Ha! That is as honest an answer as I have ever heard, especially from someone who does not yet know who he is."

"I also experienced loss and profound grief that seemed to come with the love, and no matter what I did to just focus on the love, nothing ever worked; I still felt so much grief."

"Then grieve! When there is nothing you can do but grieve, then grieve. Love is still there; it will wait for you.

"But I digress somewhat. Where was I? Ah yes, expectations. To believe that something should or should not be creates the expectation and reality that something will be or will not be. There are also judgments behind these expectations, such as the judgment that everything else is less real, less important, less correct or valuable. When you judge that someone is smart, are you not looking to see that what that person says is in agreement with your point of view?"

"Well, of course! Intelligent people are ones who mostly agree with us, aren't they?" said Adam, a little tongue-in-cheek.

"Uh huh. Is this not what the ego-self does to maintain separation and dominance? The ego-self is a right-making machine. Even if you think you are wrong, you are being right about that. Can you not see how this limits your access to reality and anything new?

"You made yourself detach from the experience of love because its loss was so painful. You then attached to a belief that love would only bring pain, having loved and lost so many times in your short life."

How did the old guy know all that from just my one-word answer? mused the boy to himself.

"To be attached to your beliefs, biases, and expectations leaves you closed to the here and now, and it is only in the here and now that you have access to magic. Anything that takes you out of the now, such as an expectation built from decisions from your past or a fear of some nonexistent future reality, will take away your access to magic. The truth is that the past and future do not exist, do they?"

"Well, the past is no longer here, and the future hasn't happened yet, so you're right; they don't exist. At least not now."

"Precisely! 'Not now.' So, what is left is the now, and if there is only the now, where is that ubiquitous thing that there is never enough of? I mean time. A good friend once asked me, 'Where did yesterday go?'"

"Seems like nonsense to me," muttered Adam.

"It does, does it not? Today it is here, tomorrow it is gone—but where did it go? How come you can never get it back? Does the past always determine the present and the present determine the future? And why does time only appear to pass? Are there other realities where time does not move in a singular direction?"

"Not in this one; that's for sure! And does it really matter?" mumbled Adam once again. His mind had stopped following the magus's backward and forward line of enquiry and froze into the safety of the here and now.

"Without the bookends of past and future, all you have is the eternal now. It is there that you will find the magic. It is from this magical place that you can journey through the eternal. It is only in the now that you can experience love, and it is only through love that magic can happen.

"Humans have a funny relationship with time in that they believe that it moves and that it only moves in one direction—from past to present and from present to future. But to twist a phrase given to me by an old friend, 'It is a poor sense of time that only moves forward.' Time does not actually move at all, for there is only the present moment, and all the moments—those you call past, present, and future—exist simultaneously in this present moment. When fully conscious of this, you can see the connections between the three spaces of time and how they influence each other."

Adam pondered this when the magus seemingly changed the direction and point of the discussion.

"Do you believe in a heaven and hell, either metaphorical or real?"

That's a funny question to be asking now. Why does he careen between ideas like that? mused Adam. "I believe that I can experience either of them here on earth but won't rule out the possibility that either can be a destination after I die."

"Ah, hedging your bets, huh?"

Adam shrugged his shoulders and grinned.

"Because there is only the here and now, both heaven and hell, love, and hate, exist within you at this very moment. Let that seep in, my boy, for there is power in knowing this, because you determine across every moment of the eternal now in what space you are going to be."

The old wizard paused for a moment, seemingly looking for an answer to what he wanted to say next.

Suddenly the whole concept of the eternal now came rushing at Adam. "Wait, Wait, What? Did you just get rid of time?"

And there was his answer. "Yes, and if time and space are, as my friend and fellow wizard Albert suggested, two sides of the same coin, what happens to the coin if we get rid of one side?"

"It … it doesn't exist?"

"Precisely, yet again! Such a bright young man. You are both old and young, wise and foolish. The experience of time and space that you have been conditioned to is not a hindrance to your journey through it."

"But that means that you've also gotten rid of reality."

"But only the reality you thought you knew," finished the magus, feeling triumphant.

"But ... but then how do I know reality? How will I know what it looks like?" pleaded the young man.

"When you choose it! But that is too simple an answer."

But to Adam this didn't sound like any answer at all, and his mind began to swim and swirl randomly while he desperately tried to grab some solid thread of a thought he could anchor to. Indiscriminate images whirled and whorled about, taking and losing form as he tried to focus upon them. All moved like thickened liquid and climbed the sides of his mind, only to be pulled back into its muck. He could just make out the magus talking and willed his mind to focus on the words.

"... when all about you, you see mystery, when you are moved by wonder and awe and your eyes are alight with joy, it is like skipping rocks across a river and drawing hearts with your finger in a foggy mirror; when graces, miracles, and epiphanies appear without warning and you never have to apologize for your wildness, when falling in love and everything makes you smile and your heart swells in your chest, then you will know something about what reality looks like!" exclaimed the old wizard rather cryptically and with a lopsided grin, as though he were seeing and feeling something very special.

Then, with hardly a breath taken, he began again. "When you look at your dreams, what do you see? Do you not see people flying or walking through walls, shifting scenes across great distances with no means of transportation, or swimming some great sea while breathing underwater? It seems like magic, does it not?"

"It does, yes. But aren't dreams just illogical images floating around from the day's debris?"

"That is your waking state interpretation by the ego-self. When you sleep, that ego-self part of your psyche is moderated, and its highly rational and linear perspective and point of view on reality becomes detached and is put on hold. Dreams are metaphors of the psychology of the dreamer, just as myths are allegories of the psychology of the cultures that create them. Dreams are your personal mythology unfolding. There is something special in the place from which dreams unfold. It is a place where invisible patterns can be seen, and your waking reality can be decoded. Do you know what that special energy is?"

"Magic?" proclaimed the boy tentatively.

"Precisely! Your dreams are like a vision that will provide you a means of letting go of all your waking world attachments to an illusory reality and magically draw aside the veil between you and what is real. You, my boy, will have two significant dreams and two powerful visions during your time with me. These four together will be messengers from your deeper spirit; heed them well."

"What do wizards dream?" asked Adam facetiously.

"Things that would send cold shivers down your back and wake you screaming in the middle of the night."

Never too sure as to whether the old man was yanking his chain, he thought better of exploring the magus's statement any further.

"Now, let us get back to what I was talking about regarding your lack of detachment, which seems like your life mantra up to this point. What you have done up to now in your quest to let go is to engage one of the very same tools the ego-self uses to separate you from reality—that is, your expectations and judgments. You just exchanged one set of attachments for another. I said to detach from everything!" cried the magus with a slightly raised voice.

The boy just stood there, gaping. "But I thought—"

"That is the problem; you are still thinking. You actually think that your thoughts are important, do you not?"

"Yes, sir. But now I'm beginning to wonder."

"Stop befriending your thoughts; stop acting as though they have any real contribution to the wielding of magic whatsoever!" he demanded emphatically. "They are worthless when it comes to magic. Just let go of everything, even your silly little thoughts! We will talk about the usefulness of thoughts later, after you have learned to let go of them."

All the boy heard was the phrase "silly little thoughts," which he then repeated aloud defiantly.

"Do I detect pride? Have you become the thought that your thoughts are not silly? Foolish boy!" proclaimed the old man as he taunted the young man without mercy.

The boy clenched his hands into fists and could feel the heat of anger crawling up the sides of his neck and onto his face. There was a *scintillae*, or sparkling phantom light, that rose from the depths of his being and morphed into a dark shadow that slithered its way forward and enveloped him from head to foot, constricting all light and reason. His head throbbed and his heart pounded.

As he was starting to lose conscious control of himself, words of fear, threat, and rage spit like flames from his mouth—words that he had never heard himself say before. What had been shadow creatures had morphed into demons of fire.

This couldn't be him speaking. And then it struck him, hard, as though he had been hit by a bat across his forehead. Momentarily he swooned. His expectations, pride, and anger were taking over. It was as though the shadows of the fire demons had risen from the darkness of the deep well of his unseen self. They were in control and were beginning to dominate everything. Not only was he attached; he was literally joined at the ego.

With great effort, he confronted his anger, feeling every constricted effect upon his body and mind. Memories rushed to the surface of the indignities he had had to endure, both physical and psychological, from his mother's death and the betrayal from so many in his life and how it had hurt every time and so often that he swore he would never let anyone hurt him again.

He had been carrying so much anger, hurt, and resentment for so long and had stuffed it all so deep within his unconscious, where he thought it would all disappear, yet here they were again. They were always there, never permanently buried, and, like some zombie or some venomous snake coiled beneath a rock, were all too ready to strike when he least expected it. All too often, these buried memories would cause feelings to flame and engulf him.

But this time he just let them be and began to relax, watching the flames fade away as he did so. In so doing, he was taking away the fuel the fire needed to continue the flame and letting the fire of his ego slowly extinguish. There was fire, but he was not the fire. The judgments that fueled it were deemed imaginary and no longer of him. Finally, he found his own voice again. "This is … isn't as easy as I … as I thought," he stuttered.

"Nothing worth being or having ever is," sighed the old man. "Your heart is sad. This is not the life you would have willingly chosen, but it is the one you have. You are learning that acceptance of reality is rarely an easy task and that overthinking it seldom helps to deal with it. In fact, too much thinking gets in the way of being magic. But if you want to get to the place where the magic lies, you need to get outside your thoughts and let your soul move you. When you fulfill the wants and needs of your soul, the connection with magic opens up."

"Can you give an example?"

"Have you ever had something inside of you speak to you just below the threshold of awareness, almost as an intuition that presented you with a feeling, insight, or premonition?"

"Well, yes!"

"Did you follow it?"

"Not always."

"When you did not follow, how often did it prove true?"

"Frequently!"

"You might want to give traction to that deeper voice a little more often. This is not a curiosity or something to be taken lightly; it is the magical voice of your deeper self that is always available if you give yourself the ears to hear and the openness to trust.

"This is what world-class dancers, musicians, artists, actors, poets, and writers do. They each bring the mystery of reality into our awareness. During creation they transcend the ego and let their souls guide them. I think they call it 'being in the zone,' but by whatever name, it is in this space that the magic will find you. Stop trying to control and let that which animates you guide you.

"When you step outside tonight, take a moment with your eyes closed and greet whatever is there. Feel and listen to the world around you. Then go home and wander around in your thoughts for a while. Do not try to change them or not to have them; just notice them as they wander through your mind. Notice what happens in your body when they come to visit and what other thoughts enter the conversation in your head.

"I want you to be an observer of your thoughts and feelings throughout your day, not a participant. Observe without judging or figuring out, or predicting, or labeling, or being distracted in any other way. Just watch them. If at any time you notice that you have gotten caught up in them, acknowledge them and go back to observing without judging yourself.

"Basically, I just want you to get out of your head.

"Try to see and feel with your heart. The head has its place in the realm of things, but you now want to transcend the world of things. The things you observe are not there. These things are just possibilities—that is, potentials. It is you who makes them real. It is your heart that reigns in the greater world of the spirit, not your head."

"I can hardly let go of my head!" blurted the boy facetiously.

"True that! The head is about reason, science, control, defensiveness, and protection, all of which are very necessary to live in the world effectively, but they can also put up walls to magic.

"The heart is about vulnerability and an opening of the door to magic. Heart is where there resides the divine impulse to become aware of relationships that connect everything to everything else. By doing this, you connect with all those aspects of what seems like separate experience and can see how they relate to one another.

"In the heart lies the bigger you that chooses reality, and it does this all the time. It is this part of you that I want you to find and open to. It is in the heart where you can see the role you play in all your experiences.

"There is so much that you cannot see when you are looking through the fog of your undisciplined mind. It is only when you see through the clarity of your heart that you can see the unseen. But you must surrender the head's need to protect itself, because while in this mode one reinforces the separateness that limits the magic.

"As long as you are in your head, you are bound up and unable to see the reality around you and the part you are always playing in its creation. You create without knowing and take no responsibility for it, but when in the heart, you become part of the creating force, and it is in this mode that magic comes to be."

Adam sighed. *Here he goes again with the creation bit.*

"You will want to ask yourself what role you play in the reality around you. Is it just a disconnected and separated God that determines the reality of your experience? Or is there an aspect of your deeper self that plays a role? What is that deeper self? What is your relationship to it? Is it one of equality or subservience?

"The head has its place in the world of the objective—that is, the separated world of things—but it is in your center where you will find your connection to the spirit of all things. It is in this most mysterious center that you will find the true meaning of salvation—to become whole again.

"There will always be times when you are in your head no matter how hard you try to stay centered, so when you find yourself back in your head, I want you to imagine what can be, because that broadens the realm of possibilities and potential and encourages you to always be looking around the next corner.

"Imagine having a mind like that of a baby or young child—a beginner's mind, if you will—a mind that embraces nothing but the moment. Try to approach every experience as though you were a child having its very first contact. Be curious and live in the incomprehensible. The already explored and comprehensible is of the small self—the limited self. Why explore what you already think you have visited? This is the process of regaining the immense energy and wisdom of the child."

"I've known of a lot of childish people that had energy, but it was negative energy that did more harm than good," said Adam disdainfully.

"I want to be clear that the child within is not the childishness of the ignorant, arrogant, immature, and self-centered mind, for the child of which I speak is that of the divine and knows the ultimate knowledge of what he or she is, is as old as the beginning of time, and is imbued in everyone and everything. Though it can be aggravating to adults, this energy of the child is essential to the enchantment of life.

"To this inner child, the world is a mythic place with something that most grown-ups, whether they follow some religion or not, have lost touch with. For most of us, we have lost touch with the mythic world of our birth.

"Within every child is a meaning and purpose that over time is thwarted and buried by the conditioned process of becoming a grown-up. Over time, an unbalanced tension between the child's real meaning and purpose and that which is laid upon him by the culture creates a disconnect between the conditioned self and the real self. Because humans, like all other organic matter, are self-regulating for the purpose of maintaining a healthy balance, the tension needs to be resolved. It is the process of balancing chaos with order, child essence with adult essence.

"Though resolutions can be positive and balanced they can also be negative and lead to dysfunctions. Even positive resolutions in one context can become negative in another and these dysfunctions can lead to a cutting off from the magic that is all about us and limits our soul expression in the world."

"But what if I do it wrong? I've always had trouble doing things in the right way," interjected the boy, who desperately wanted to learn the way that was being offered here.

The old man smiled at this and then gently suggested, "It is only the ego-self, that made-up self, or the child-self that has been made to feel inferior that worries about whether it is or was any good or not.

"I want you to especially observe your expectations. There is no expected outcome for this exercise. Whatever you do is just fine. There is something that flows through everything, and it is restricted only through the imposition of meaning.

"Let go of the expectation that if you were to practice rightly, if you were to achieve ego detachment, that you would be a better person. You would not; you would be the same as you have always been. This process is not about getting better or being better. This is not about better. Magic is not better. Also, there is no meaning in this exercise; that is an attachment to meaning. Just do it, for no reason, and take what you get.

"Do this for a week, then come back and see me."

Adam nodded sheepishly, and with a little disappointment as to how little success he was having, he turned slowly toward the door. For a moment he was devoid of thoughts, but he then turned and said, "Thank you," with more earnest gratitude than he had ever experienced before. The old man smiled, for he knew that the acknowledgment came not through a thought but from the very soul of the boy himself, and for just that moment the room lit up brightly.

CHAPTER 4

Torment, Dissolution, Recombination, Transmutation: The Alchemical Mysterium

This heart will glow no more! Thou art a living man
no more, Empedocles! Nothing but a devouring flame
of thought–but a naked eternally restless mind!
To the elements it came from everything will return.
Our bodies to earth, our blood to water,
Heat to fire, breath to air.
They were well born; they will be well entombed.

—Mathew Arnold, from *Empedocles on Etna*

"*Well?*" *queried* the wizard, waiting patiently for him to speak.

"It has been a week of tears of joy and sadness in almost equal measure. I've had insights that broadened my understanding and those that seemed to crush my very being. I have touched the face of God and have been burned by unspeakable evils. I feel as though I'm not what I was, having transformed myself both now and into the future and deep into the past. I am profoundly grateful and so very resentful of what you have done to me and now feel lost and alone in the world that was once my home. And what's worse, I fear that I no longer care about your stupid magic."

"A bit dramatic, are we not? You will have to change this self-pity. You will need to learn to let go of that part of yourself, for there is no magic in that. I suspect you probably feel justified in feeling sorry for yourself. Get over yourself! Be sad if you must, but do not let the sadness be who you are.

"Now, listen to me well, boy, for I am about to reveal the rest of your curriculum that only now can you comprehend. You have entered a cleansing, or dissolution, stage of your transformation—a transformation that is necessary for you to attain your true spiritual inheritance. Once you have entered, you cannot turn back, for to do so would leave you at best dead or worst dissolved and no longer able to function properly. Hear now what it is you need to do to reclaim your birthright. Are you ready?"

Adam stood there, and despite some misgivings, he was ready to absorb what the wizard was sharing. He nodded his assent and then cleared his throat. "I'm listening, though my fear grows by the second. And even though I can set it aside and watch it grow without becoming it, I wonder for how long this body and soul can endure."

The boy was struggling to control himself and remain centered in the bigger self he had discovered during his practice of the week before. He hadn't been aware of it then, but he would need all his strength to make it through the transmuting gauntlet he was about to experience. As the wizard invited him to sit in the chair next to him, he sunk down and then straightened and slid to the very edge of the seat, barely in the chair at all, and focused everything on the old man who sat before him.

"Your body—mind included, for I am not of the popular notion that they are in any way separated—is an instrument of magic. But like any instrument, it can become useless if you haven't taken care of it. Over time you have gunked it up with so many ideas, rigid beliefs, illusions, fantastical expectations, thoughts, and worthless and fake items of knowledge that it can barely fizzle, let alone sizzle or sparkle. Forget about using it to create the space consciously and intentionally for magic, because the natural flow from the source to the greater reality of the self is impeded by all the accumulated crap you have attached to it. Do you understand?"

"Now who's being dramatic? But in answer to your question, so far, yes, I understand," said the boy as he gestured for the old man to continue.

"We will see. What we have been doing is scraping off this crap so as to polish the tool once again and give it the purpose for which it was designed. After that you will relearn the art of using it properly."

The old man paused and thought a moment before speaking again. He then absently picked up his pipe and took a drag, tapping it against the bowl when he realized it had gone out. Looking toward the ceiling, he raised a hand, and an odd-shaped brass pipe tamper with a squatting Elvin creature affixed above it appeared, whereupon the old man used it to tamp down a new infusion of tobacco. When he let go of it, it hovered for a moment before disappearing.

The wizard then pulled a match from a container next to the bowl and held it for a moment, and the match flamed without being struck. He then put the flame to his pipe and relit it. As he took a couple of drags, a faint glow emanated from the pipe bowl. After another drag, he leisurely exhaled a puff of smoke that created a ring that floated above his head. Meanwhile the young man just sat patiently, waiting for what was next.

Holding the pipe by the bowl, the old man pointed the stem toward the boy and went on with his lecture. "Your body is the *prima materia* that needs to undergo a tormenting cleansing to be transformed. As it is now, it is like lead—heavy and without luster. It needs to be sublimated from something base into something of greater value. This will require a complete transformation from the ordinary to the sublime, from the cursed to the sacred, and from the unconscious to the conscious.

"When you have completed this process, only part of which you have been practicing this past week, you will shine like gold and take a step toward being whole once again. After that you will learn to transcend the body and no longer *be* it but include it within your greater sphere." He paused to see whether the boy was still focused on what he was saying, and after satisfying himself that he was, he continued.

"The body must be consumed by fire, dismembered, and dissolved before it is re-enlivened and made whole again. Though the process of living can act as a crucible where one will burn in preparation for the transformation into a more brilliant being, the process takes too long—sometimes many lifetimes."

As the wizard paused and took another drag on his pipe, the young man couldn't help himself and made a comment. "Wait, what? Consumed by fire, dismembered? Is this for real? This sounds like the ravings of an alchemist!"

"In that you are right, but their so-called ravings were the metaphorical process for transforming the dull leaden consciousness of humankind into the bright golden spirit that humans were born to be. The alchemical process, also known by the practitioners of the art as Chrysopoeia, is the process of becoming a whole self and being fully what we are. What we are is love, belonging, communion, and connectedness.

"The truth for each of us is that within us is a metaphorical philosopher's stone, a lapis that holds wisdom and youth that can bring a vitality to our being. But to forge it into reality requires a precise tormenting of the prima materia and a great synthesis of our disparate parts. It is our own *elixir vitae*. One must transcend the body to bring about the communion necessary for magic to appear."

Frustrated with the words that the magus sometimes used, Adam intervened. "You originally said that magic was not about Latin-sounding words, and yet you keep using Latin in your descriptions. Why is that?"

"This is a sacred and holy space whose purpose is to focus the energy for the transformation that is about to take place. Here you will be dying to the way you have been."

"There are some concepts better communicated through the old language of the alchemists who discovered the process over two millennia ago. Can we continue?"

Partially satisfied with the answer, Adam nodded his assent. It did bring another question to mind about how old the magus must be, but he decided to table that thought for later.

"One must dissolve one's image of oneself; that is, one must let go of the ego-self and clean away the persona that person and the culture have created that masks the true self. When one exists as separated self, the belonging that we all crave cannot come to be.

"Like the baptismal water of your youth that cleansed you of your sins, the alchemist's fire will help to cleanse away the vestiges of your ego-self and the masks that you wear to protect this false self. This will be your first of four rebirths before all is done."

Abruptly he stopped and became very serious in demeanor, focusing his full attention on the boy. Adam squirmed in his seat at the discomfort of the old man's penetrating gaze.

"Do you trust me, boy?"

Trust? This was not an easy task for Adam, given his history of feeling betrayed by people—mainly his family. But this magus was not his family. He had not transferred his lack of trust to this man. As he sat perfectly still and looked within to see whether indeed, he did trust the old man, he found that he did, and he declared unequivocally, "Yes, sir!"

"Good, then stand up. The time has come for the crucible of fire known as the Torment."

The Torment? The boy shuddered at what was next, but the old man hadn't hurt him so far. In fact, his administrations had opened him to a world he hadn't even known existed before now—a world of exquisite emotion and revelation—and he was anxious for more. Besides, hadn't he always been his own torment? How much worse could this be than all those years at his own hand?

"Before we can make room for the new, we must first destroy the old, *solve et coagula*," declared the magus. "In order to reunify the illusory dichotomy of the qualitative versus quantitative aspects of being, this will be the first of a number of processes you will be going through. First, we will draw a circle upon the floor." He made a slow clockwise motion with his hand in front of the fire, and a faint, almost imperceptible, blue-white glow appeared upon the rug before the hearth. Several shadowy specters stood around the perimeter of the forming circle.

As the magus continued the circle toward its close, the shadow creatures began to stir and fly about the room, making whooshing sounds as they flew by objects and the two people in the room with them.

"What are those?" cried out Adam as one flew toward him and then careened around his legs, leaving them chilled in its wake.

"They are the unfinished and discarnate souls of those who failed to come back from the fire," said the magus, indifferent to the whooshing of the flitting phantoms, for he had seen this spectacle many times. He had never been sure whether the creatures were rooting for the neophytes' success or their failure.

"Sheeit, what? Failed to come back from what?"

Adam stood there as though glued to the floor, terrified of what was about to happen but resolved to see it through. After all, it was only metaphorical and not real, right?

As the old wizard completed the circle, he placed his hands upon Adam's shoulders and looked him square in the eyes, demanding that he focus on his every word.

"This is a sacred and holy space whose purpose is to focus the energy for the transformation that is about to take place. Here you will be dying to the way you have been. Here you will be entering a new spiritual dimension the likes of which you have never imagined. Stand within the circle and before the fire with your arms stretched out perpendicular to your body like this." The wizard stood with his arms outstretched and his feet spread apart, forming the five points of a pentagram. Adam did as he was told. "Stand quietly and let the energy of the house be absorbed within you," asserted the old man, who moved one hand to gently touch Adam's forehead. With this Adam fell into a calm and deeply receptive state of consciousness, whereupon he then complied and moved forward.

"Let go of your thoughts and walk into the flames," directed the wizard as he reached over to again lay his hand upon the green book still sitting on the side table.

Once again, he saw the tiny fire creatures, fairies really, beckoning him toward the flames. The young man trembled and was aware that this would have been foolhardy on his own or with anyone other than this particular old wizard, but for some reason he knew that this man had only his best interests at heart, and he walked slowly toward and into the fire. It was warming, welcoming, and felt like the right thing to do.

Dissolution (Sol Niger—The Black Sun)

The fire fairies swarmed around him, grabbing, and pulling at his clothing. Suddenly his pants caught the flames, and before he knew what was happening, a vase-like apparition seemed to surround him. Without warning he was engulfed by the fire. The heat became unbearable, and pain rapidly grew beyond the threshold of endurance. At first, he felt his skin crackle, slough, and begin to melt from his body. His pulse pounded and his breath quickened, making it difficult for him to breathe. As it took his external body, the fire seemed as though it were being liberated from within him as well.

"Oh my God, I'm going to die!" He screamed a most bloodcurdling and wordless scream so big that it nearly caught in his throat but broke free, ricocheted off the walls, and then trailed off to a pitiful whimper as he passed out and fell headlong into the flames, becoming a human torch that lit up the entire room. After a short flare of intense heat, what was left collapsed and quickly turned to a pile of blackened ash. The specters had perched themselves in the rafters, watching intently like vultures upon some high flung aerie. The sickening burnt-liver smell of barbecued human flesh and sulfur filled the room and caused the old man's stomach to churn and his face to grimace.

As the smell cleared, the room become deathly quiet, with only the memory of those tortured screams remaining. The wizard then returned to his chair and casually picked up his pipe and relighted it with another match. He stretched and lay back into the softness of the chair.

He had taken many a neophyte to this point in the process and knew that for some it ended here, what with the purity of their essences having been too compromised to withstand the dissolution and then their souls not being able to master the recombination. There was also the possibility that he could be one of those where the house was being a bit cranky and did not remember the subject after he or she was gone or got some part of the equation wrong when putting him or her back together. That did not happen very often, but it was ugly when it did. Oh well, there was no help for it now. He would wait to see whether the boy was one of those. He hoped not, as he kind of liked him, but it was taking longer than usual.

Recombination: A Phoenix Reborn from the Ashes of Its Former Self

On that thought, the magus waved a hand over the ash pile in a motion that looked as though he were trying to twist the very fabric of space. A numinous and melodic sound of tuned chimes and voices, barely heard at first, began to work its way up the harmonic scale and then, both heard and felt viscerally, filled the room with a chorus of music announcing the purification of a soul. The house was singing and stirring the air. The ashes whipped and swirled into a small twisting vortex, sucking up the pile of rubble into a small tornado-like twister.

Caught in this whirlwind, the being called Adam, who had lost his body to the flames continued to struggle to retain some control over what was happening to him. He imagined he was dead but wasn't ready to give in to that. Being dead was not an option for him. *Besides*, he reasoned, *how dead can I be if I am still thinking?* He reasoned that Mr. Descartes must have been right. *I must be here if I'm still thinking.* This thought helped Adam refocus his energy from one of flailing to one of being intentional.

Anyway, there wasn't much to see in this nothing place; there was just a lot of empty—and not the kenotic empty that leads to fullness and love, but an empty of nonbeing, purposelessness, a sort of nowhere kind of thing. In this place there was not even the dark, shadowy ghostlike images he would see when he closed his eyes just before sleep. *Pretty boring.* He decided that he didn't want to stay.

While the ashes were being drawn up into the vortex, something weightier began to form, and like a phoenix being reborn from the ashes of its destruction, the form of the boy came into view, at first insubstantial and then slowly hardening. The perching specters began to fade.

The music had once again, as it had so many times before, saved a soul in peril. The old man never tired of this part of the process, remembering fondly his own rebirth from dissolution to recombination.

And as quickly as he had been destroyed, the boy was once again whole, naked and glowing before the fire. As the music faded away, a reformed and transformed Adam turned toward the old wizard with a spark in his eye and with love flowing out from every pore.

"Wow! That was incredible! Wow!" Adam shouted as he looked down at himself and touched his chest, looked at his hands both front and back, and shakily ran them along his upper thighs to make sure he was all there.

Transmutation: From Lead to Gold

"There is a robe in the cabinet over there," suggested the magus as he leaned forward and pointed to an armoire appearing from the dark at the far end of the room. Adam crossed the room, seemingly without ever touching the floor with his feet; motioned the cabinet to open; and donned the robe. He returned to the fireside tying the sash around his waist.

Adam was still so full of energy he could hardly contain himself. He was like a five-year-old boy waiting to unwrap Christmas presents under the tree and having been told to sit still while the adults talked—a task all but impossible. But forever Mr. Practicality, the magus brusquely brought him up short.

"You must be hungry. Newbies are always born hungry. I will whip up a grilled cheese and some tomato bisque." Up he hopped, and he strode into the kitchen. In no time at all, Adam could smell the melted cheese and hot tomato wafting through the room.

"God, I am hungry!" He said just as the magus called him over. It was the best grilled cheese and tomato soup he'd ever had, though on second thought he realized it was probably the only grilled cheese and tomato soup he'd ever had. Between bites and slurps, Adam shared his experience with the fire, occasionally stopping midbite when a missed memory crossed his mind and he wanted to back up and share that too. The wizard just smiled all the while, for this was Adam's special moment. Soon enough the sharing came to an end, as did the food; and as the old man placed all the dishes in the sink, he began to talk.

"You will need to rest now, for there is much more work to be done to fully reinvigorate the psyche and bring it out of its dream. You can sleep in the next room if you like," he said offhandedly while flicking his hand in the direction of the bedroom.

"You could suck the joy out of Christmas," accused Adam.

"Christmas? Yes, met him once, good man! Now *he* was one who could see magic. Here, take this and place it under your pillow; it will help with your dreams and fortify you for what lies ahead," asserted the old man as he pulled a sprig of yarrow leaf from the air and held it out to Adam. "When you wake, we will cook up some breakfast." He motioned to the heretofore not seen bedroom in the house, and the boy, suddenly feeling incredibly exhausted, took him up on the offer. Upon entering the room, Adam barely noticed the glow of a large white crystal cluster sitting upon a side table with a note attached to one of its spires. *This will not do; I can't sleep with all that light.* He walked over to it and removed the note. On it he read, "For your healing and sleeping, leave me beside you throughout the night." Deciding that he could live with it for one night, Adam shrugged his shoulders and left the crystal glowing. *Why,* he mused, did *the house seem to know what its boarders or owner needed?*

Meanwhile, the old man settled back once again into his chair. He was barely conscious of the rattling of dishes and pots in the kitchen as each washed itself and stored itself away. He sighed in relief. "I am glad he made it. It is always so difficult to explain a disappearance to the authorities when they do not," he said reflectively as he smiled broadly.

CHAPTER 5

The Twelve Laws of Magic: A Magical Canon

Nothing real can be threatened. Nothing unreal exists.

—*The Course in Miracles*

Come morning, the young man, wearing the robe he had donned the night before, staggered out of his room and into the parlor slowly, scratching himself here and there, trying to bring feeling back to an unconscious body. There, sitting serenely and staring into the fire's enduring maw, was his mentor. "My God!" he groaned. "Do you never sleep?" Barely able to stand upright, he groaned again, "I feel like hell, woke all twisted up in the sheets, and fell out of the bed while trying to untangle. All night I dreamed of being split in two from head to foot while boiling water was poured over me, scalding, and searing my flesh. Try as I did, I couldn't force myself awake until I watched my head split open and a beautiful golden orb fly out. What horror is this, and what does it mean?"

The *Anima Mundi* (World Soul)

Slowly the old man placed the omnipresent pipe into the tray beside him and turned to face the boy.

"Dreams can be a masquerade for the real us that hides within. They are important communication links with our deeper selves. Because they are not of the superficial mind, the conscious mind and ego, they deliver messages from the unconscious part of the self that often views reality in such a way that, if accurately embraced through personal reflection as to meaning, can open the door to the magic that lies deep within every one of us. They are part of what is needed for us to step out of our separation and to become whole. The symbols of the dream are like the symbols of the waking world but without the interference of our conscious and conditioned mind and all come to us in the aid of our health and well-being.

"The world that you see in your waking state has been corrupted by the conditioned mind. In the subjective experience of us all, there is another reality every bit as substantial and valid as the objective world, though this has, for the most part, been rejected by a science and society built on separateness. As I have said before, magic cannot exist in a world based on separateness.

"Everything is infused with the spirit and its magic. The trick is to transcend the mayhem of the conditioned mind and to reconnect with the primal unity of reality.

"When in the waking world, we tend to interpret through that part of our conditioning that can skew the real meaning. There is a magical technique, however, for working lucidly with a dream while still in the dream."

"Can you teach me that?"

"In good time, my boy, in good time. However, for now, if this were my dream, for I can only speak for myself and not you, it would mean that transformation is not quite finished. Though you are not of your original substance, you have yet to release the nous within, the soul, which is what we call the *Anima Mundi,* the soul of the world.

"An old friend of mine once called it the over-soul, or the soul of the whole. It is the place within which your true being is contained and where we all mix and become one. For thousands of years, humankind has searched the libraries of the soul without being able to resolve its true meaning or its true source.

"It is the source of humankind's and your own individual genius. It is what propels you ever forward and is the energy behind all magic. Until you have released this creative source of your being, you remain earthbound and subject to the ego. Until then, you remain separated from your true being.

"Go take a shower and release the soul. Wash away that which separates you from all else and begin the journey the divine intended all of us to take!"

Adam slowly turned and walked back into the room where he had slept, disrobed, and climbed into the shower in the alcove at the far end of the room.

The Cleansing

Turning on the shower, Adam began his ritual bathing, but before he could soap up, the water became unbearably hot and scalding; the nightmare that had been his dream was coming to be. It had become so hot that he felt his skin begin to melt and to flow like mercury slowly circling the drain below him. Again, the smell of sulfur permeated the room. He opened his mouth to scream, but only a yellow liquid came out, and it covered him all over.

After a short time, the pain stopped, and he began to feel a warmth that seemed to wash away all the aches from the night before. His body had turned an unhealthy bright red. Then, as quickly as it had happened, everything seemed to return to normal—but a much more relaxed normal. He could smell the clove-like scent of carnations as he brushed his hands along his arms. It was a nice smell, a healing smell that magically seemed to banish from his memory the pain that had overwhelmed him just moments before, bringing with it a bristling of energy.

As he looked down at his half-outstretched arms, they seemed to glow with health. It felt as though every part of him had been reborn. And indeed, it had, but no longer as the individual separate from all others; instead, as something a little more inclusive of the whole of the world.

"This is great, but I could do without all the pain and drama," he said to himself.

He did an outward inspection of his arms and turned his hands from palm to back and inspected his legs and torso, which seemed to also glow with health rather than with the burns he had felt just moments before. An inward inspection revealed that he felt great, better than he had ever felt before, and he stepped from the shower, got dressed in the clothing magically appearing upon a chair just outside the shower room, toweled his hair, and, leaving it wild and unbrushed, walked out to the main room feeling invigorated and famished as in really hungry, as though he had been fasting an eternity. "When do we eat?" he growled eagerly. "This transformation stuff makes me hungry."

Together the magus and the young man prepared a small but adequate feast of lentils flavored with chopped onion, along with some colorful herbs the boy had never heard of. In fact, one cupboard was filled with herbs the likes of which he had never heard of. They then added a crisp salad of many strange leafy greens, sliced mango, and a red cabbage.

Mysteriously, ingredients seemed to appear in the wizard's hands as needed and then disappear when no longer in use. Cleanup was never an issue—something he would discover more than once while living with the magus.

Still hungry after consuming all that, the boy asked if there were any eggs he could fry up, and the magus reached into the fridge, pulled out a box of eggs, and handed it to the young man. Breaking an egg into the iron frying pan used to fry up the lentils, he laughed and exclaimed, "Would you look at that—two yolks in one egg! I wonder how often that happens?" Shrugging his shoulders, he added another two eggs and what was left of the onions to the pan.

"In the old days," said the magus, "it was said that two yolks were an omen for having twins, but clearly you and I are not having twins. It was also seen as auguring a life-changing event where two things would become one in someone's future."

"Gee, superstitious much?" declared Adam as he scooped the mélange onto his plate and sat down. He offered to share with the magus, but the old man demurred, already full of the earlier fare. But he sat with Adam as he ate.

After consuming most of it, they sat down before the fire and sipped a cup of freshly brewed coffee to begin their talk about the day's proceedings.

The old man blew across the rim of the cup to cool it down and took a sip. "Whoa, that is a little too strong!" he exclaimed to nobody in particular. "I am not a bloody marine, you know!" In response, the room seemed to sigh. The magus took another sip and smiled. "That is better."

Behind them Adam could hear the clatter of dishes and the metallic clinking of silverware, and he turned to see what was making the racket as the last glass neatly stored itself in the cupboard to the left of the sink. But before he could reflect on it, the old man began talking.

"What you have been doing up until now has been training your mind to give it some discipline. You need to do this, so your mind is an aid and not a hindrance to being magic. A mind caught in the self-centered chaos of the ego-consciousness is worthless to the practice of magic. Do you understand?"

"I do, yes."

"Good! I am going to present you with the twelve laws, well, gates really, of magic and give you an opportunity to practice each until you and I both are satisfied that you have mastered them and are able to open to the magic. Are you up for that?" As Adam listened, he nodded and noticed that the wizard had changed his tone, in that he was now addressing him as an equal instead of the one-down relationship he earlier experienced. It felt good; he felt confident and cheerfully looked forward to what was next in his training.

"Now I must warn you, we do not have much time, and we are running out of it, and there is a lot to be done," offered the old sage with an air of urgency in his voice.

The Ouroboros Dragon: An Alchemical Symbol for Completion and Wholeness

"Running out? I don't understand."

"We have spent the last few weeks calling forth the four spirits of water, fire, air, and earth, but now we must complete your development before the slaying of the dragon." The old man pointed toward a crest affixed to the hearth. On it was a carving of a dragon coiled in a circle and biting its own tail.

That's odd, thought the boy. *I hadn't noticed it before.* "What does it mean? The coiled dragon, that is."

"The serpent is called an Ouroboros, a Snorgon of great power, and represents magical energy that is the spirit energy that lies deep within our animal selves. The transformation that must take place for one to wield magic is, in its broadest sense, a dragon's tale. But unlike the stories of the giant worms of the ancient Celts, this Snorgon is not a demon of power whose guile is said to have stirred up the mother of humankind, but a daemon, a benevolent spirit.

"She represents transformative spiritual energy—what is known as the kundalini, or 'the coiled one,' which resides in each of us. She is also symbolic of the dormant energy that can release humankind from its bondage of ignorance of the magic that is their essence and their birthright. To the ancients, she also represented infinity, healing, unity, and the ever-enduring birth, death, and rebirth cycle of existence. The alchemists used it as a symbol of both the beginning and end of their work.

"In this case, she is slaying herself, but she is also embracing herself that is her real self, and in that she represents the integrated whole. She is eating herself because she receives her nourishment not from something outside herself but from within—a necessary condition for transformation. To be open to the magic, you must not eat of those outside of you but only of yourself."

"I was taught that it was a symbol of evil."

"The symbol is both good and evil, representing both life and death, healing, and resurrection. Unfortunately, some Christians mistook this symbol in the negative of one's soul as a demon, and because of this, for many, its true power was lost.

"It has also been said by the ancient Norse wizards that when the snake lets go of his tail it will be the time for one's current world to end and a new world to begin. Your daemon snake is about to free itself and bring the … no, bring *your* end with it."

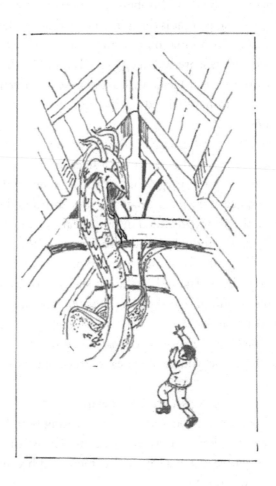

"… it reared its scaly and heavily muscled body and rose
high into the rafters, snorting a stream of fire."

"There are many hidden artifacts and meanings within the fabric of older houses such as this. They are often ritually concealed by long dead owners to protect or pay homage to the spirit of the house. Sometimes without warning, they can reveal themselves to us. They can come through its walls, cellars, attics, and fireplaces. This house is notorious for doing that." There was an ominous tone in the old man's words.

It was then that Adam noticed a sparkle that seemed to rise from below as though from a dark, hidden well beneath the floorboards. He couldn't tell whether it climbed through the floor, from the abyss, or from the primeval chaos within him. He had seen this once before when it seemed to herald an impending change in awareness. The spark settled above the hearth, where the dragon carving suddenly became animated and uncoiled itself.

As it grew rapidly in size, it reared its scaly and heavily muscled body and rose high into the rafters, snorting a stream of fire. Bending its terrifying head downward, it opened its fearsome jaws, and with teeth gnashing and nostrils flaring, it let out the most frightening, bloodcurdling scream as it dived downward toward the cowering boy.

Its head was covered in small hissing and writhing snakelets like a medusa's crown, and Adam could feel the beast's hot, wet breath searing the back of his neck and soaking his clothes. Its long outstretched tongue, which preceded its downward thrust, lashed across his face, leaving a nasty welt. Though crouching and barely able to keep his feet, he mustered enough resolve to turn and face his tormentor and confront it openly. It was as though the waking world universe was forcing him to own up to and face his demons and turn them into daemons.

But before the impending oblivion had time to consume him, the dragon disappeared in a puff of smoke as quickly as it had come, leaving the boy half standing, shaking, and dripping with sweat. Quickly he pulled his wits together and calmed his breathing as the magus had taught him. He reasoned that it was only an apparition of his fatigued mind, or maybe he was losing his mind, but with a shudder he shook the vision off and cautiously straightened up.

"What the hell was that?" he demanded of no one in particular.

"Looks like you were having fun."

"Being nearly eaten by a dragon isn't nearly as fun as one might think. It even tried to toast me beforehand."

"That was very creative."

"You mean of me?"

"No, the dragon. Most just like their food sushi style."

"Oh ha, ha, very funny."

"Not to worry. It has probably returned to its place within the house, having announced its presence and given its energy to you."

"Its energy? It almost ate mine!" said Adam, still somewhat indignant at how the house seemed to act toward him.

Without answering, the old magus's tone changed, and he became most serious in his intent. "Let us get back to the issue at hand because the time is drawing nigh. It is ordained that on the fifteenth night of its fullness, this month's moon will rise new and yet rival the sun. We are twelve days into the prophecy, and there will be an eclipse of the sun on the third day hence. Upon the sun's rise, each of the orbs of the prima materia will consume themselves, the union of your separates will come to pass, and the magical lapis will be forged within you. What was split asunder will come together again. This is when the conscious and unconscious worlds within you will join and when the light of consciousness will leave the field of birth and death.

"Once you have completed your education, your conscious mind will be ready to absorb—that is, embrace—the contents of the unconscious, wherein your magic lies. This absorption will be initiated by the coming together of the sun and the moon of the eclipse. It is the process whereby a mature psyche is born, and it is only through the kind of person who has been reborn in this way that magic can happen. But if your conscious mind is not ready to assimilate, you will be caught between these two forces, and the energy produced by the chaotic fragments in the unconscious will cause disorder and madness, even death—death of the body possibly, but even worse, the death of the soul. So many have had their bodies leave them before they have recovered their lost soul. So many have caught themselves up in the spiritual wasteland society has created that their souls have been at worst lost and at best hidden."

"Spiritual wasteland?"

"Yes, we are all living in a neurotic world of anxiety, anger, despair, addictions, spiritual emptiness, and meaningless goals that have robbed us of our natural selves, our core being, and our ability to see and access magic. What you and I have been doing is dissolving the negative aspects that have obstructed your ability to recover your soul and become whole. Once you started down this road, you had no choice but to be ready for this event."

"Would have been nice to have known that ahead of time," muttered Adam half to himself. "Well, no help for it now; we had better get on with it then," he said with a slight edge to his voice.

"Right! These basic laws of magic are deceptively simple, so do not be fooled by what may seem to be obvious. Magic is born from mystery, as are all things like art, religion, and science. All are born from mystery. When one thinks that one knows something, mystery dies and nothing new can be born. It is in the marveling at the world within and about us that we can access our bigger selves. Without it the eye dims and the soul dies. Are you ready?" The boy nodded, though internally he wasn't ready at all.

"Can I take notes?" queried Adam as he reached for his cell phone.

"Typical student type! No, the taking of notes would get in the way of understanding in the present moment. The taking of notes is too much of a distraction. Just be with what I am saying. Ask questions if you must. If you do not understand now, you never will. This is not like committing to memory some formula. You will remember it when the time comes to use it. So put that thing away."

Shrugging, Adam stuffed the cell phone back into his pocket. As he did so, he had the rather disconcerting thought that his phone was an anomaly, simultaneously existing and not existing. Was there even such a thing as a cell phone? What an odd thought! He reached again for the phone that didn't seem to be there and then checked his watch. Time was playing tricks with his mind again. Was it the house shifting or just his experience of things? At any rate, all seemed odd in this space. Once again, the mentor's words pulled him out of his reverie.

"The first law states that magic is all around us. We are already in it; we are already it. There is no place where it is not, and no creature lives apart from it. It exists in a space where there are no boundaries. Who and what we are is magic. Magic is always our companion if we have but the eyes to see it and the heart to walk with it. But humankind in general lives within a delusion that hides the magic. But it is there, under every rock and branch, every pool of water, and every soul that walks the earth.

"The realization of magic does require that you cast off your current delusional ground of being and be open to your real self—your whole self, your unified self."

Hesitantly Adam raised his hand, and the magus nodded to him. "Ground of being? I don't understand."

"Good, you are someone who cares more for the subject than how he looks. Too many so-called students just sit there acting as though they understand when they have not a clue, hoping only to maintain an illusion of smartness. But they are looking in the wrong place for their smartness.

"The reality of magic and one's ability to see it is like the concept of figure-ground perception." The magus then held up a piece of paper and declared, "I can see words, the figure, on this piece of white paper, the ground, when the words are black." Words appeared on the paper as if summoned. "The less the contrast between the words and the background, the more difficult it is to see them." The words began to fade upon the paper.

"Now imagine a reality where the words are all black but written on black paper." As he said this, the paper turned black. "All one can see is blackness, and the words do not seem to exist. But they are there. This is like the unenlightened mind whose conditioned ground of being is blackness, and the reality of the word is like magic; it is there, but against the ground of being of a blackened mind that has been conditioned to see only black, one cannot see it.

"To solve this problem, either the figure or the background needs to change in order to see the magic. However, magic is immutable—but the mind that sees it is not. Therefore, it is one's ground of being—or thinking, or experiencing mind—that needs to change.

"Magic is neither black nor white, so the analogy could just as easily have the words be white on a white sheet of paper, but the same property of the mind needs to change," he offered as the paper disconcertingly shifted rapidly from white to black and back again several times. "There needs to be a change or shift in perspective to see what really stands before us—to see what is really happening, what is really there."

"But things happen to us; no shift in experience can change that, can it?"

"Ah yes, this is where my example plays out in the everyday. Expect the unexpected. Everything that happens, happens *for* us and not *to* us. Making that slight shift in perspective from 'to' to 'for'—that is, from a ground of being of something to overcome or avoid to something to embrace and grow from—can make a powerful difference in opening the door to magic.

"Through this magic we moment by moment create reality by what we focus on and by what we conjure in our minds, whether we are awake or dreaming. The very act of dreaming is magical, and as much as waking life is but a dream, it, too, is magical."

"Wait a minute, what do you mean waking life is a dream?" asked the young man incredulously.

"How do you know it is not?" asked the Magus.

"Well, I … well, I … uh, well, I guess I don't, come to think of it."

"And how do you know I am not dreaming you instead of you me, or that you are dreaming me dreaming you?"

"Well, I'm not sure of anything now. I guess right now I could just be dreaming I'm awake and having this confusing conversation."

"That is certainly one possibility, but there are some very wise people over the centuries who have suggested also that we are but a dream and that the life you live is but a dream and that it is only when you awaken that you can know your true meaning."

"But how will I know if I've awakened?"

"When you are no longer dreaming."

"Now I'm really confused!"

"Of course, you are, and that is what humans do. They lose their focus and allow themselves to get captured by some irrelevant and unimportant trivia with no real answers and then wonder why they are confused. My fault, really. My poor choice of words led you astray. I do that a lot, been working on it for ages." The wizard ran his hand across his forehead and over his hair to the back of his neck as though to help him refocus.

"Do not let yourself get bogged down with all that. Just ponder it for now, for it is unimportant now as to the reality of whether we are but a dream. Just know that your idea of what is real or not, or what is magic or not, is of little consequence to the reality that magic is everywhere and to what magic really is."

"Right! The first law."

"You need to stop your mind from getting hooked by trivia such as what reality is. Adam, *you do not know reality.*" The magus emphasized each word forcefully. "However, if you allow yourself to get stuck in the dreaming reality argument—or any argument, for that matter—it will distract from what is really important. Many a would-be magus has missed his or her chance at wielding magic by getting stuck in arguing unimportant minutiae, for when arguing, it is only your personal and limited point of view that you are arguing with, and magic does not reside in your personal point of view.

"In any event, this first law gives rise to the second law, which states that magic is a way of living and is not separate from everyday experience. Who you are lives within it, you are made of it, and you *are* it. It is all magic! Once you have embraced the fact that magic is embedded in everything and everyone, and that every experience is magical, you can begin to see where it is in everything and how it manifests in all its different forms.

"You do not attain magic, though you may attain the ability to be it and see it. Look around you. Do you see in people only what you have determined is good or bad, right or wrong, or who is friend or foe?"

"A little, yeah."

"The magic exists in each of them as well, whether you label them bad or good. In the world of magic, there are no friends or foes, or right and wrong; there are just guides to the magic. Each can open us to compassion and broaden our perspective of what is possible. Each is struggling to live his or her life in the best way he or she knows how. Each is trying to find the magic in his or her life. Each of them is trying to fill the void left when his or her wholeness became fragmented.

"We all have the same spirit within us; we are all essentially of one essence. We are all magicians, if only we could just see it. Everyone we meet is an extension of ourselves. At our deepest level, there are no strangers. As a matter of fact, this is what makes it possible for all of us to exercise the power of magic."

"But there are those who would do us harm, aren't there? Shouldn't we be cautious?" asked the boy.

"Of course. There are many who do not have even the slightest inkling of who they are; nor have they any desire to discover it. They live in the dark and know not of the light or that there is any light to know about. To them it is all fantasy and airy-fairy dribble. To them life is about survival and what only they can see in front of them.

"Even their image of a greater power is confused and diluted, and their access to it is virtually closed to them. They are separated from their source and from all else. In this state, they can be dangerous to others as well as themselves. However, they represent that part of ourselves that has not found the light. They are, at their core, you and me. Their essence is still where the magic lies."

"Yeah, but—"

"There is an old Arab saying that goes, 'Trust in Allah, but tie up your camel.' Know that every man and woman is your spiritual brother and sister but be practical and do not trust that they have seen that light or have placed the same value on that connection. Yes, God is with you, but you, not He, are expected to take care of yourself and to take the necessary practical actions to care for yourself, others, and the world. You are the hands of God.

"Another way to put it is 'Say a prayer but move your feet.' In other words, in this context take responsibility for yourself. But it is not just for yourself; it is also for the whole. You cannot be a bystander in life and be able to engage in magic. Another wizard friend who wrote in the book"—he touched the book beside him—"was known to have said, 'He looked this way and that and saw no one,' meaning that you cannot just stand by in your life pretending you cannot see and therefore are not to be involved in and responsible for what is going on in it. That is how racism, misogyny, and bullying remain embedded in a culture. You are responsible for all of it."

"Boy, you're just full of these pithy little sayings, aren't you?" blurted Adam with a smile and a slow shake of his head.

"They are in the wizard's manual under 'profound and pithy sayings,'" alleged the old man.

"Really?"

"No, of course not. But you do get the point."

"Of course, I do!" exclaimed the boy a little reluctantly. "Be responsible for what's happening in your life; be responsible for what is being created in your witness of it."

"Nice! I think you got it on its deeper level as well."

Adam smiled.

"Thirdly, we have access to magic when we do not place limits upon our expression. By 'limits upon expression' I mean that people normally react to vulnerability by going into a defensive posture mentally. These defenses become barriers—barriers to what you are deep within. Expand what you are open to by embracing vulnerability, and magic will emerge. What you are is magic, Adam. Stop trying to fit yourself into what is not you.

"You look in a mirror and say, 'That is me: crooked nose, with one eyebrow slightly higher than the other, lips a little too thin.' All those judgements you have attached to yourself to identify the image. But you are not the image in the mirror or in someone else's mind, for both are smudged. Stop apologizing for your wildness. As uncomfortable as vulnerability is, it is a prerequisite to being open to magic."

Adam absently pressed his fingertips lightly against his lips as though to affirm that they were not "too thin."

"I am not including physical threat here. Defending oneself to real physical threats is most important. I am talking about ego threats, such as the threats to your pride or sense of your ego-self, or the persona or mask that you have built to protect yourself."

"What mask are you talking about? I don't wear a mask."

"The mask I am referring to is metaphorical and represents what and who you want others to think you are and what you yourself want to be but are not necessarily. It is what I call a personality mask. For example, I used to wear the mask of the good guy, thinking that this would protect me from criticism, because I viewed criticism as a denial of my worth. But I am not always a good guy, and it never really protected me from criticism.

"We also wear masks to hide what we are feeling. Some depressed people wear the mask of the optimist, while an anxious person might put on the mask of a calm person. Others will wear of the mask of a happy person when he or she is anything but happy. We use them to cope, protect, gain acceptance for, or hide our true feelings.

"Look closely at your experience with family. What decisions or judgments have you made about life generally regarding their dependability?"

"I don't know!"

"Yes, you do; look more closely."

"Well, I guess that I am cautious because people can be so undependable and unpredictable."

"So perhaps you have trouble trusting in people and life events because of being a victim to this unpredictability?"

"Yeah, I guess so."

"And perhaps you withhold yourself so as to not be vulnerable and are often suspicious of the intentions of others?"

"Yes, I, I guess that too," he said hesitatingly, as though he were wondering where this was all going.

"So maybe you wear the mask of a cynic, and this is designed to help protect yourself from the unpredictable? But has it ever protected you, or has it just separated you from others or from the experience itself and created an expectation?"

"Yeah, I get it! This would make it more difficult to get close to anyone. You're right! In all my musings and daydreamed stories, I always end up hurt and alone. I make myself the hero, but in my story the hero never feels as though he belongs, so he takes himself away. I've often wondered why I do that."

"That story or way of perceiving would then limit your access to magic. There is also a negative or critical mask that often hides the amazing parts of ourselves almost as though it protects our essence by denying its existence. This mask diminishes the expression of our essence and at the same time diminishes our power, making it very difficult to see, let alone to wield magic.

"These masks are also how we want to see ourselves for whatever reason, and they reinforce how we see the desired self. But how we see ourselves is also how and what we see in the world. Simply put, if we can see the magic in ourselves, we can then see the magic in the world."

"But how do we really know what's behind the mask?" asked the boy.

"We actually have many masks that we use at any given moment. After identifying the mask you are using at any one moment, ask yourself why you are using it. What would you have to give up taking the mask off? But in a deeper sense than this, what is it you are in awe of?"

"What do you mean?" Adam was always a little nonplussed when the magus would seemingly change the subject in the middle of a concept. It was like a whiplash of the mind.

"I mean when you see something in someone that you highly respect or are in awe of—for example, a talent or a way of being that really impresses you. Look inside right now to see how that feels."

Adam closed his eyes and tried to imagine some event or person that he was really excited about and then looked at the feelings he experienced in that moment. Connecting with feelings was not that easy for him, because all his life he had had to shove them to the back of his mind to move forward in life, or at least he had convinced himself that this was what was needed. But these were positive emotions he was searching for, so what was the harm?

"Well, it … it feels powerful, awesome, special. Sometimes my whole body feels electrified. Sometimes it moves me to tears. Sometimes those tears seem to come from loss or envy—you know, from wishing I had a talent." The young man breathed, and at this tears came again to his eyes, for all those times he had felt happiness or felt powerful and strong now seemed lost and diminished or were not a part of him anymore no matter how he longed for them.

The old wizard saw the tears in the young man's eyes and softened his approach so as to honor the boy's experience.

"What I am trying to say is that whatever you are in awe of you also are. It is what you are behind your masks. You cannot see it in others if it is not in you. That is the way you see what is behind the mask. What else are you in awe of? What else moves you?"

Again, he took some time on the question, looking through all his experiences until he remembered an event just last week in the park when watching an old man moving with obvious pain bend down awkwardly to help a young boy who had fallen on his knees while running to catch up with his bigger brother. With the boy's eyes full of tears, the man offered his hand and said something to the boy that seemed to support him, and with this the boy got up and started to run off but then turned and gave the old man a quick hug before he left.

"I suppose when I see people reach out to one another—I mean when they show caring for one another."

"When they show love for one another?"

"Yes, that's it I guess."

"When people come out from behind the mask, it is their essence that shines, and it is your essence that sees that. Behind the mask is something most magical and most beautiful. It is in those times when the soul speaks to soul. And what is the language of these souls? Why, it is love, of course.

"When you see the magic in another person, know that it is your own magic as well that you are seeing. This magic is always there; it cannot be hurt, and it cannot be betrayed. It does not need protecting. When in its loving embrace, who you are is safe and cannot be hurt.

"The energy that fuels your ability to produce magic is simply—or, rather, not so simply—love, and the self-centeredness of fear being the enemy of love chokes the life out of it."

At this point something deep inside Adam began to stir. For a moment he felt something new, and then his eyes seemed to tear, but he choked them back, not wanting the magus to see him cry—and over what ... love?

"So, what I'd have to give up in order to take the mask off is fear."

"Precisely!"

This caused Adam some discomfort, for fear had been his constant companion for as long as he could remember. Without its illusory armor, he would have to confront his vulnerability.

The wizard paused for a moment, seeing the boy's unease. Then, sensing that the moment had passed, he went on. "There are also the masks of high confidence or self-righteousness or humbleness, which are for many desirable attributes, to be sure, except when worn to hide a lack of forgiveness for another's failings or for those failings in oneself. Masks are also turned inward as a means of compensating for these imagined lacks or failures. What mask have you been hiding behind to feel better about yourself?"

The young man slowly lowered his head and silently looked within head and heart until he began to feel a rapid thumping in his chest and his hands became clammy. He was becoming nervous and a little embarrassed at the thought that rose within him. At first, he wanted to reject the thought, but he knew that this was exactly what he had always done before when something uncomfortable arose. Clearly it was this that the old man was referring to.

"I hide behind a mask of competence and self-confidence when actually I almost never feel competent or confident of my abilities. Mostly I think of myself as having no talents or meaningful contributions." He instantly felt somewhat apologetic for the admission of the hidden weakness.

"Interesting! But I think that this mask also covers up something much more serious in that it acts as an excuse for you to not be responsible for your power. You may be afraid of your power and whether others would accept you if you let it out. It is a protection and a defense against rejection, but it limits your ability to express your magic.

"Continuing to hide behind any mask inhibits or limits your access to and effectiveness with magic. Discovering the masks that you wear is a means of knowing where you are hurting so that you can administer healing and thus open your access to magic. To know who you are behind the masks gives you the power to use them when it is appropriate."

"But sometimes I have to protect myself from some of the language people use—you know, when they attack me verbally."

"But to just be protective by denying or not listening is a defensive stance that puts up walls and limits or closes down possibilities. Magic cannot exist in such an environment. Physical or psychological walls cut off possibilities and reduce the vistas of reality. Vision narrows until you see only what is in the narrow tunnel you have created, and the world and all its diverse beauty and potential is no longer available to you. You become small and limited and unhappy because the kingdom of happiness includes everything, and you have limited the everything through your response to fear. Acceptance of diversity expands your universe and what is available to you.

"A little fear, though handy as a motivator and early warning system, can be lethal to your well-being when you are constantly being bombarded with it and are continuously on alert. Your vision becomes highly focused on defense strategies or escape routes and blocks out virtually everything else. Over time it begins to wear your body's effectiveness down and causes deterioration in your thoughtful response to almost anything. In other words, under constant fear you become stupid. In this state one is very limited in what one can see around oneself, and magic is almost always the first casualty.

"Another problem with masks is their upkeep. I will bet you think that who you are is the same today as you were yesterday."

"Well, yeah!"

"Well, you are not. You are not the same moment by moment, let alone day by day. By trying to maintain a reputation, a look, or a way of being, you are wasting energy. This is the energy that you could have access to if you were to just be what you are in the moment."

"But what am I? How can I be what I am if I don't know what I am?"

"You are trying to label and define being, and you are also trying to do being—neither of which is being. Stop trying to be and just be. The doing of being limits the soul's free expression and therefore your access to magic. Open your heart and let your soul just be. There is also the experience of bliss. Magic comes through bliss, and you cannot have or do real bliss. You are either in a state of bliss or you are not. Bliss, like magic, can only be found in the space of just being.

"This third law leads to the fourth law, which says that the conscious mind can only open to magic when the soul is allowed to express freely by not limiting itself. There is a void in your soul—an empty space that can only be filled when that soul has been set free."

"So how do I set it free and open beyond my limits?"

"Firstly, you must dismantle the boundaries you have created by forgiving yourself for all that you believe you have failed at and those whom you believe you have failed. You have acted small in many ways and have sold and limited your soul for money, security, a singular and repressive belief, or through despair. You must now forgive yourself for the smallness. Who you are is perfect in every way, but the things you do and think and believe are not. Forgive yourself and others for those imperfections and the shame and guilt that come with them and weigh on one's ability. Imagining a bigger self will free you to be that greater self. Forgiveness, tolerance, compassion, and patience are all doors into magic.

"Now do not misunderstand me; the clearing and forgiveness of oneself is not a one-time only event. The ego-self continually collects the litter of human fallibility and like so many dust bunnies must be periodically swept out. We create barriers to seeing and expressing magic through harboring feelings of resentment because we have not truly forgiven that which we resent. No person can fully reconcile his or her negative acts to such a point where the aggrieved feels that reparation has been fully made. There will be no reconciliation until the aggrieved has forgiven the perpetrator."

"But some things can never be forgiven!" cried Adam.

"What you mean is that some acts can never be right but will always be wrong and that those who do the wrong must be held accountable. Is that right?"

"Yes, of course!"

"Forgiveness is not for the perpetrator of the misdeed. It is for the aggrieved. It is the means for letting go of the anger and grief and reconciling with reality. It is one of the only ways of removing this great stumbling block to magic.

"Once the heart and head have been cleared of this debris, you must then call upon the prophets of imagination. Imagination is a powerful tool. It is the creator of all the works of humankind and of their gods as well. It is through the power of the imagination that the divine spirit can embody itself into our world. What could be more powerful and magical than this?

"Imagining what can be or imagining another way to be or do something is the precursor to all that there is. Imagining broadens the realm of possibilities and encourages you to see not only what is around the next bend but also what is right in front of you.

"The root of all humankind's creations begins with their imaginings and creative fantasies. It is our inner fire that transforms the desire of the divine spirit, the heart of us all. So honor the imagination, for it is a serious precursor to magic.

"When you do find yourself in the realm of your thoughts, be creative in your thinking and less rational. Be a little impulsive and less reasoned. Too much cause-and-effect reasoning can stifle creativity, and creativity cannot be found in a box with rigid boundaries.

"Magic is timeless and is not to be found in the past, which is gone, or in any future, which does not exist. It grows out from the moment by moment of the now."

"But there is a past, and future isn't there?" asked the boy, trying to smooth out his confusion.

"Of course, but not in the paradigm that you are used to. They all exist as one and can only be thought of individually in the present. It is only the conscious mind that separates the temporal into these categories of experience; otherwise, you would be experiencing everything at once, and that would be very disconcerting." He smiled at the thought.

"Like any mechanism, the mind is subject to momentary hiccups or breakdowns; those moments are when one can see the future in the present. It is by knowing when this is happening that you can then take advantage of it.

"Basically, though, the subjective ego-mind does not like the now and adopts either a future position of 'someday when' or a past position of 'if only it had been.' But life and its magic are happening in the present. To be anywhere else misses the magic. In short, be where you are; be here now. It is only in the now of being that one can hear the secret language of everything. Listen to the rain when it is raining, the wind as it blows through the trees. And in the silence of the night, when embracing the now, you can hear the stars twinkling. It is a language that needs no translation when you are truly listening.

"Be fully in the moment of everything you do and everything you experience. By not being in the now, you are functioning out of a subjective protest to what is, and the 'what is' does not care about your protestations.

"In the now—that is, the present moment—there is no fear, and it is only in the moments of now that you can find the eternal, nontemporal calmness you need to be magical. But it is very hard to be present to the moment when you are letting your chattering mind carry you away from it."

"That's like the old saying that goes something like, 'Still your mind and know.'"

"In a way, yes. It is part of a biblical phrase: 'Be still and know that I am God.' It can bring peace to the fearful and chattering mind, and for sure when one can quiet the mind, one can be open to what is around and within oneself. And when one can do this, one is also open to magic.

"I have used this phrase as a prayer and means to center myself and clear the fear that clutters my mind so that I can actually see what is before me."

"How so?"

"Well, this is as good a time as any to introduce this centering technique. Goodness knows it will probably come in handy many times in your life. But I caution, one needs to do what I am about to tell you with great intention. During any inward process, the mind will wander and drag your consciousness away. When you notice your focus being diverted by some thought or outer directed distraction, do not go with it; notice your loss of focus and just let it go without recrimination and start over. Do you understand?"

"I do. Though it's not easy."

"True, it may take several tries. The small-mind consciousness has been conditioned to rattle on and distract you from the here and now. The practice is a means for transcending the small mind and moving into the larger mind. This move opens the mind and increases its receptivity—a necessary condition to realizing magic. At the end of the prayer there lies a mysterious something that reaches out, comforts you, and takes you in. Are you ready?"

Adam nodded his assent.

"Silently repeat the following eight lines of prayer, leaving off the last word of the previous line until there are no more words to recite. For example,

"Be still and know that I am God.

"Be still and know that I am.

"Be still and know that I.

"Be still and know that.

"Be still and know.

"Be still and

"Be still.

"Be.

"Sit up straight, close your eyes, and as you travel down the scale toward your center, permit yourself to go deeper into the quiet place within you by allowing each layer of your mind to quiet itself until you arrive at the 'Be,' and then just be."

Adam sat upright, and after slowly closing his eyes, he began to recite the prayer in his mind as instructed, and by the time he arrived at "Be," all had quieted. He had never felt so calm and so open to reality.

The old man waited several moments and then quietly asked, "Are you ready to continue?"

Adam smiled and just nodded, not wanting to disturb his silence.

"The fifth law states that magic cannot be controlled or done; in fact, one must release control to wield it. Learn to stop 'doing' so that you can experience 'being.' In short, practice 'being.' That does not mean that you should not 'do,' but you can 'do' within the conscious place of being. If the context of your life is about doing—with not-doing, thinking, trying to understand, and trying to figure out being other forms of doing—magic is rarely experienced, and life becomes ever more of a struggle. Even your quest to learn about magic is wasted effort given that if you can just be still, the magic will find you. Magic dwells in the silent places within your heart. The magic you are looking for is also looking for you. It has always been there, waiting for you to show up.

"Your life is like a container of all things. Make your life about being, and then place within that container all the doing, and your life will be transformed. Th—"

The old man was interrupted when the boy cried out, "That's silly! How can I do magic without actually *doing* it?"

"Ah yes, that does seem contradictory—a real paradox, as they say— but magic is about being, not doing. You cannot understand, know about it, or control it because those are 'doings.' Magic does not come from understanding, because that requires reason and magic is unreasonable. Magic arises on its own and not through your manipulation or wishing it. Thinking that you can manipulate something through magic is just magical thinking, not magic.

"You are either it or you are not. Do you understand?"

"Not really."

"Uh, Adam, I can explain, but you have to do the understanding," said the magus with just a hint of frustration. Adam just shrugged with a slight sheepish grin.

The magus paused as though to collect his thoughts and decide which direction to go in with his presentation. After a moment, he began again. "Magic is not like waving wands, casting spells or charms, mixing potions, or invoking some religious ritual, though some of my brethren have suggested that our mind–body structure acts as wand for the soul.

"It is like an intention, and that is a state of being, not a doing. You can have an intention, but all the doing in the world will not actualize it unless you yourself have become the intention. Oh, you can still use wands and cast spells, but only in the context of intentionality and as a means of consciously focusing that intentionality. The use of these devices and rituals can, in the context of enlightenment, transform the energy within the magician and make it possible for him or her to manifest the magic. The focusing of intention quite literally affects outcome in what appears to be a magical way.

"By 'focusing' I also mean that you are doing what you are doing intentionally in that you are intending a certain outcome. Focus is always the most important factor in the actualization of an intention. When your focus wavers, so does your intentionality. Have you ever noticed that when you have your unfocused attention on something other than what you are doing, you become more vulnerable to errors: stubbing your toe, cutting yourself with a paring knife, hitting your thumb with a hammer, or any number of such mistakes? This happens when we have lost our focus and intention, and often our bodies suffer."

Adam recalled a time when he was always in such a rush that he was constantly stubbing his toes against chairs, tables, and the like. He also knew that when he slowed down and paid attention to what he was doing, those painful intrusions happened much less often.

"We are the creators of what we see when we become intention. In a world captured by illusions, intention made manifest by the right use of free will and action—that is, in the space beyond ego-dominated motivation and awareness—is where true magic lies. Again, magic is about being, not doing. Properly expressed intentions and being are not doings."

"But I've intended a lot of things without anything happening," exclaimed the boy plaintively.

"No doubt you have, and that is usually the best way of knowing whether you truly intended something," asserted the old man, ending with a bit of a chuckle.

"I don't understand."

"You know whether you intended something if it actually happens. Intention often comes from some desire that is something you want to have happen, so you make it your intention to make it happen, right?"

"Well, yes, I guess so."

"Often our desire gets muddied through the mix of competing desires regarding the same issue. For example, you may want to get into a relationship with that redheaded barista at the coffee shop, but at the same time you do not want to make a fool of yourself. The stronger of those two desires will often win out. I should also point out that the need to protect oneself is a barrier to the kind of intimacy that is needed to experience magic."

"We talked about this earlier when talking about the effect of my cynic's mask."

"Precisely!" the old man exclaimed with a certain amount of pride in his voice.

Adam's mind traveled out to the coffee shop and the sight of Sarah working behind the counter, and his heart jumped, and a warm feeling mixed with a little anxiousness came over him. *Now how did he know about her?* he wondered to himself. He then blurted, "How do you do that? It's like you're reading my mind."

"When you can just be with another person, place, or thing, you can then connect at a level most people have not the slightest idea exists. When you can transcend your beliefs, judgments, prejudices, and self-involvement, you can connect with people in a profoundly connected way."

"Is this why you are able to sometimes read my mind?"

"The simple answer is yes, though it is not your mind I am reading. But again, I digress. Now where was I?"

"Something to do with Sarah—you know, the barista—and manifesting desire," reminded Adam.

"Oh yes, it is funny how mentioning the barista focused your attention," claimed the wizard with a wink in Adam's direction that was met with a shy shrug and a grin.

"Secondly, when you have become clear about your desire, that is when you are clear about the reality you want to create; you need to then access your free will. That occurs when you are accepting of either a positive or negative outcome. Couple this with a purposeful action, and then intention can manifest."

"But how am I to be sure that my desire is clear?"

"First of all, it is not just about desire; it is also about your emotions. Emotions can affect the actualization of your intentions. Ignorance of your emotions can thwart an intention as much as mixed and competing desires. Altering an emotion through the conscious act of becoming aware of an emotional pattern, such as with the anger that exists in you, and looking for its opposite, in this case, compassion, you can see another potential reality. Coupled with true free will, you can then choose which emotion is appropriate to the situation.

"What I do to increase my awareness of the patterns of desire and emotion in my life is to meditate on them and to scan my body to see where these emotions have taken residence, but I also pose the question before I fall asleep and let my dreams provide an answer," offered the old man. "Both dreams and meditation can offer hints at right or purposeful action as well.

"When one changes one's conscious attitude toward something, such as changing the negative thought that you always get tongue-tied and fearful around a pretty girl and inevitably look foolish to one of being more focused on her, then the engagement with the girl becomes less one of fear of how you might look and more an interest in getting to know who she is. This will alter your reality of her, and your intention will be manifest.

"Your desire is to get to know her, so be your desire. How you look while manifesting it is of no consequence. This will also increase your ability for compassion, which will ultimately connect you with everyone and everything that is a necessary condition for performing magic."

"Yes, but how do I do this being?" implored Adam, and then he stopped, and a broad smile of recognition came across his face. "Probably not by doing, I assume?"

"I think he is getting it!" exclaimed the old wizard aloud to himself. "This may be a difficult concept for those who tend to see the world literally versus metaphorically, concretely versus abstractly, practically versus whimsically, or inside the rules box versus outside the rules box, or for those whose default response to dealing with problems is to 'do' something. Men are especially prone to this. For now, just be open to the possibility of another reality and restrain the urge to 'do.' 'Doing' will come later.

"If you want to know magic, watch children play. Watch the pure unselfconsciousness in their frolic. Watch them just dance when they are dancing, paint when they are painting, and sing when they are singing. Listen to their unpretentious description of the mysterious world around them.

"And that is the sixth law, in that magic cannot happen when the consciousness is on itself. When the small self is constantly projecting itself onto everything and everyone, reality becomes a function of those projections and confuses one as to one's real self and the reality around oneself. The continual focus on self prevents seeing reality as it is, to the point where one can no longer tell sense from nonsense."

"But you need to be aware of what is missing in yourself in order to get it fulfilled, don't you?"

"Self-centeredness is not self-awareness. One needs to be open to one's own scrutiny and to tell the truth about it. This can only happen when one lets go of the self: the small self, the fearful self, the 'reasonable' self, the striving and unfulfilled self—the self that wants to look good, or to at least not look bad.

"When one has one's focus on oneself, one cannot see the 'other,' whether that other is another human being or the things in the space around oneself. When one cannot see the other, one cannot see one's true self, for it is in the other that one can get an awareness of oneself.

"When one is focused on one's own survival—one's own supposed needs and desires—there is a constant agitation of striving to get and in not losing what is gotten. But what is really lost is the awareness of our essence. What is lost is the calmness that comes from truly knowing who we are. What we lose is the fact that we are magic.

"One cannot find the calmness inside when one is focused on the survival of the ego-self, and without the calmness, one cannot be magic. Without the calmness, the pendulum of life swings wildly, and this prevents access to magic.

"The striving for fulfillment of the self-conscious mind disrupts awareness and misdirects it to something that magic is not.

"The self-conscious mind is always seeking pleasure and, of course, avoiding pain both physical and psychic. This is what leads to addiction, striving, and avoiding. Both are psychological in nature but can lead to physical addictions as well. Both are often governed from the past, and both have strong feeling tones attached to them, and that is something that can obstruct self-awareness and self-control. It is as though something other than either the small self or the greater self is running the show.

"When addicted to anything, whether it be an idea, an act, or a substance, the 'I' disappears, and the person vanishes. This can lead to a false sense of wholeness, but wholeness is not wholeness without the 'I'—without both the smaller and greater selves.

"Both the self-serving acts of striving and avoiding are also often, at their root level, a desire to be at one with the spiritual—that is, to become whole. But these behaviors actually separate one from the path to wholeness and therefore limit access to magic.

"In the seventh law, the concept of separation becomes clear when one understands that magic only becomes available when one dissolves the separation between one's opposites and recombines them into a functional whole."

"That's what you've had me doing all this time!"

"Precisely. You needed to let go of that tough, assertive personality whose power is faint as compared to the power of your greater spirit. It is the divided ego that you needed to render. You needed to learn to dissolve your conflicted inner gender aspects and to integrate both sides of yourself because your assertive, decisive, active, thoughtful, exclusive, inclusive, rational, irrational, powerful, forceful, creative, compassionate, emotional, and intuitive sides can all coexist without conflict in that they are mutually supportive. They are actually one thing.

"In your Western upbringing, you have been taught that everything is either/or, black or white, you or something that is not you. You have been convinced that to be good you had to reject bad and, in some cases, do it with violent suppression of what is deemed bad. Have you ever noticed that this suppression not only does not end the bad but often increases it or causes something even worse?"

"Can't we just learn to tolerate each other?"

"Is not that just another form of suppression?"

"Well, I can't just let bad be; there will never be peace and justice if we don't at least rein it in," said Adam with just a little disgust in his voice.

"Learn to see not only the evil in the world but also the evil in yourself. You need to comprehend your own darkness, just as the darkness needs to comprehend the light. Both must be fully cognizant of the other to reconcile—that is, to coexist. In short, one needs to make room for the dark. This will always be a struggle. That which brings peace only to the individual is not peace. Manipulating a mental image of someone or something so that you feel at peace with him or her or it to not have to look at your emotional unrest is a false peace."

It was true that Adam had done a great deal of mental gymnastics trying to make the people who had abandoned him in life be okay in his mind so he could be at peace with them. But the pain and anger were always there, waiting to strike.

"Use the dark side as a road sign for where good resides. Be aware of your own dark and aggressive urges, and do not turn them onto the 'other' by projecting them onto the other as though they were the other's alone or acting them out on the other by attacking him or her. Learn to see when you are acting out of your dark side.

"When tempted to express the dark side, there are simple wisdoms passed down through the ages that can help, and they should never be held lightly, for they are much more powerful than you could ever imagine. Some examples of these are the Golden Rule, the commandments, seeing yourself in others, loving others as you love yourself, and the idea that what we do to everything we do to ourselves. These are acts upon evil and upon each other that produce powerful magic.

"Even the philosophies that embrace a mixing grayness contrast this to that which is not gray. It is only the limited mind of the ego-self that takes sides and holds steadfastly to one way or the other and allows only one set of aspects to be dominant. In most belief systems, truth is said to be 'the way it is,' but, because we can never know what anything really is, the truth needs to include what something is not as well. Little, if any, balance can be maintained in a separated ego or sustained in a bifurcated self or belief."

Separation and Coagulation

"But everything in the world is separate!" interjected the young man.

"True. In the accepted version of reality, we are separate from each other—you over there and me over here. Not only are we separated from each other and all other things, but we are also separated within ourselves. This is to say we are not fully integrated.

"We maintain this separation to maintain our self-importance. Lose your self-importance. Self-grandeur is illusory and is used only to protect you from your fears. It is the small, terrified ego that needs these illusions of protection to give it some sense of control—of which, as I have said, there is none. In this state, the healing power of the psyche cannot be accessed.

"To be able to heal oneself or to wield magic requires that one give up this dominance of the ego-self. However, most people will make all kinds of Faustian deals to maintain the dominance of their egos. Politics is rife with this; people give up their values to maintain their domination over that which they fear. But this only reinforces the demons that separate them from their magic."

"But we need to protect ourselves from all that will hurt us, don't we?"

"What are you protecting yourself against? Loss, scarcity, death? What if death is not an end but another beginning? Why, then, the protection against it? What if your perspective shifted to death being the creator of life instead of its end? Death is always with us; it defines life, for goodness' sake!

"What if you were to see loss as the midwife of gain and that not having is a bookend to having? You speak of the need to protect yourself against hurt. Your hurt has been mostly about loss—the loss of love. But too often the best protection against the loss of love is to not love, and to not love is no protection at all. We cannot protect ourselves from life, Adam. The best way to protect against life is to live it as fully as we can, to engage it, be vulnerable to it, battle with it, and struggle and embrace it—but never to dominate it.

"The drive for dominance also comes from a vision of the reality of scarcity that belies the reality of abundance. What would happen if you were to come from the perspective of already having it all?

"You can see how this perspective of scarcity plays out in children with siblings in how each vies for the attention of the parents as though there is not enough attention or love to go around. This struggle goes on without end through life in all our interactions with others, and there is no end to it because there is never enough, yet the truth is that there is always enough.

"This insatiable drive for dominance shows up in even the simplest of forms in society. You have a saying in the Western world that suggests that the least important person is on the bottom of a totem pole; I am referring to 'the low man on the pole.' But the native peoples who carved these totems often thought of the lowest figure on the pole as the most important. It is all a matter of perspective because of the perception that it is the base that holds up the top, not the other way around; but in the Western mind, it is the top that supports the whole. What an odd way of viewing things—that is, backward.

"They were also images of kinship group or connectedness commemoration and not necessarily statements of nonconnected dominance. This desire for dominance that is so strong in your world also wastes the energy needed to see and be magic. One cannot hear the magical body when listening only to the chattering fears of the ego-self. In short, trying to be first has separated you from everything, including yourself, and magic cannot exist in a condition of separation, divisiveness, and self-importance.

"For example, the masculine and feminine aspects of being that exist in all of us to one degree or another—the unconscious beliefs of culture and our individual egos, the personality aspects that we accept and desire, and those personality aspects we disdain and reject—are perceived as inner separations and are all there to help maintain the dominance of our individual egos. These separations then appear to fragment the wholeness of the human psyche and compromise the magic of the spirit to act through us."

"The feminine aspect? I don't know that I have one."

"Ah, but you do, my boy! Do you remember me talking about yin and yang energy? Well, this is what is called yin energy, and in its positive form, it can be revealed by one's openness, receptivity, and flexibility, which you have shown since the first day we met. The yin also nourishes self and others and is forgiving of personal shortcomings and those of others. Your personal struggle as an individual is to learn how to balance your masculine and feminine aspects, including the positive and negative ones. It is here that your ego-self will find its safety, and when feeling safe, it will open itself to the healing magic of the psyche.

"Being an individual does not mean that you are separated from all others, because a fully integrated individual is indivisible from the whole. One becomes whole when one becomes the greater whole."

"Isn't that just like a tautology—one is whole when one is whole?"

"Look who has the big words! No, wholeness includes the integration of all one's parts not only within the psyche but outside the psyche as well."

"You've used the word 'psyche' so many times, and for a while now I assumed you were talking about the totality of the human psychology, but there seems to be something more to it than that."

"Indeed. Psyche is the instrument of how you perceive and experience reality. It is also what is creating reality. It is both timeless and spaceless, cosmic in nature, though we tend to view it as a fabrication or, at best, a psychologist's construct. The truth is, we and the world exist within psyche's dream, inseparably united, though in our state of consciousness we view its wholeness as separate entities.

"Opening to magic requires joining these disparate parts of oneself both within and without so as to heal these separations. As separated beings, we cannot see the magic that is in everyone we meet and everything we see, feel, or hear.

"In the state of consciousness where we see ourselves as separate from everything else, we are blind to other states of reality. This point of view creates expectations that reinforce errors of our reality.

"It takes an altered state of consciousness to see into the invisible world around us. We can achieve this by accessing the imaginal realm of consciousness, where the symbolic, mythological, and archetypal landscape of the unconscious mind resides.

"We have lost the magic of 'being' because we have lost much of the art of imagining, and magic arises from the imaginal.

"In short, we can access magic when we dissolve the separation between the various parts of ourselves. The truth is that to be magic, we must be as whole as possible—or at least be working effectively toward this wholeness. To the degree that we attain wholeness is the degree to which we can practice magic. Those of us who become more authentically ourselves—that is, the more whole we become—the more magic we can be."

"Authentically me? I don't understand. I'm authentically me—no one else. I mean, I am what I am, and I don't try to be anything else."

"Not even when you wear the mask of the cynic?"

"Oh yeah, huh!" Adam quipped, remembering their earlier talk. "Funny how everything weaves together."

"You think? What I mean by 'authenticity' is being real without pretentions. It's hard to be authentic when you are doing what you do for acceptance or are trying to meet someone else's expectations—even those you think of as your own. The ego-self must be right, look good, be acceptable, and avoid rejection, all of which are barriers to authenticity. This need for acceptance might breed pretentiousness and create masks that are worn to give the impression of authenticity.

"We have to dare to be our real selves no matter how scary that may be, and to be real means to be vulnerable, which is the condition for belonging and for love, courage, and creativity. When your goal becomes about safety, you cannot be vulnerable, and you miss out on most of the joy that is available in truly belonging.

"Perhaps you need to 'share' your true self—even the self who is pretentious, self-righteous, biased, sometimes prejudiced, sometimes needy, and often self-critical. Perhaps you need to share your struggle to overcome these barriers to expressing who you really are.

"You need to share your authentic self to be real. All too often, we avoid our struggles for fear of being vulnerable or not looking good, or to protect us from nonacceptance. Not all struggle is without merit. Embrace the struggle. Struggle is like a fire to the metal beaten by the blacksmith's hammer upon the anvil. It makes us pliable to change."

Walking the Ridge

"The road to authenticity and wholeness can be unsteady and fraught with danger. Some have likened it to a narrow tightrope-like trail along a sawtooth mountain ridge with drop-offs of a thousand feet on either side, where strong and unpredictable winds buffet you unmercifully. It is safe to say that most do not make it. But if you want to get from where you are now to where you want to be, you have to 'walk the ridge.'"

Thinking that the magus was probably referring to a metaphorical wind, Adam interrupted, "What do you mean by winds? How will I recognize them?"

"Many of these winds will come from those around you; the world, in all its many wonders, will often distract you and send you off course. There are those who will criticize you because you have left the accepted and conditioned path.

"However, the greatest wind of all comes from the ego-self, the demon within you whose voice you are constantly listening to, that promises everything but gives nothing. It is the loud voice within that complains and demeans, criticizes, and leads astray. It is that voice, when given substance, that will blow away the holiness seeker—that is, the wholeness seeker—convincing him or her that the goal is unreachable or unimportant, unreal, or unsafe, or that the seeker is not good enough or deserving enough. It can also redirect to a false goal and lead one so far astray that one loses oneself."

Another Albedo Process

"These demons, or shadow selves, will tear at your soul, work beneath your conscious mind, and undermine a lot of your good intentions, scattering you to the winds. You need to call these demons out, which brings them into the light, thus taking away their power. By calling them out, you can then accept them as they are and then, without becoming or embracing them, release them and forgive them."

For a moment, Adam harkened back to when he got uncontrollably angry at something the old man said about his silly thoughts, and he realized that this had been a function of his shadow self. It was starting to make some sense to him now.

"Do you remember earlier I mentioned that you needed to be open to your feelings and not hide them? In the same way, you need to grapple with your demons—that is, your shadows—many of which reflect psychic wounds that have not yet healed. These are wounds suffered as a child and from the loss of your mother.

"You try to heal these wounds either by covering them up or by projecting them onto others."

At this Adam screwed up his face in disbelief.

"Yes! All the negatives that you apply to others live within you; otherwise, you could not see them in the other. Unrealized and not dealt with, this natural human process of shadow denial separates you from your true self and the magic that lies within.

"This is the shadow world of the unconscious self, where one must venture to become fully human. But know that venturing into this wilderness of the unconscious mind is fraught with danger, for this is the ancient wilderness that is a wildness *within* all of us and not *of* us. In that forest primeval, both mysterious and familiar, one risks crossing over the border between the wild and the tame, the human and the divine. This is a place where the supernatural roams unrestrained.

"Rejecting or trying to dominate this wildness courts becoming a false being. Essentially you need to tame the shadow not by dominating it but by taming your relationship with it. In short, you need to connect with it and integrate it, because that will provide the necessary energy to be the magic."

"You've spoken of this wildness before, magus, but I'm not sure of what it is you're speaking."

"It is the place where the primordial images of your ancestors' dwell and influence many of your actions. It is the place within which powerful ideas arise and where your masculine and feminine personalities reside. It is the place where the unified-self lives, but it is also the home where the shadow creatures lurk. These creatures represent your sexual drives and the forms they may take—repressed ideas and memories, weaknesses, desires, and instincts. Here you need to eat the lion rather than to allow him to eat you. You need to devour your animal self so that you become it and not it you."

"Sounds like a scary place to me—a place I'd sooner avoid than confront," said Adam as he shuddered.

"You and just about everyone else. But you need to discover the courage to not run from these shadow aspects but to engage them and start a conversation with them, because your shadow-self, or shadow demon, has knowledge that can illuminate your life. You are fortunate in a way because you did not drug yourself into a numbness designed to hide you from these shadow demons, though you were going through your life in a barely conscious or intentional way.

"In your case, the emptiness you felt because of this behavior is what brought you to my door. The shadow self is you as much as any other part. It is you at a lower level of consciousness. You must learn to conjoin both the sides of light and dark to be magic. Darkness is where the light can come from, in that you see the light because of the darkness. Without it you are blind."

"But how does one do that? How do you even find them if they're hiding in the shadows?" asked the young man.

"It is not easy trying to ferret out one's shadows or demons, because they are in that part of the psyche that is unconscious—in other words, that part that one is unaware of. So, what to do to bring them into one's consciousness?

"There is an ancient invocation that goes, 'As it is above, so it is below, as within, so without,'" he asserted as he once again patted the green book next to him. "This is more a reminder than an invocation, really, because it tells us that we can find out what is inside by looking closely at the outside. This is because we are always projecting ourselves onto the outside world. For example, if we want to see our shadows, we can look to see what or who disturbs us, or what we reject. This is easier to do if you can place yourself somewhere between the two worlds of the conscious and unconscious, which are both reflections of the one world."

"This makes sense in that it's one world made up of any number of conflicting parts, most of which we don't even know about, right?"

"Right! It is like a tree that has its roots in the underworld and its branches in the heavens. The branches do not know what the roots know, and vice versa, but neither can live without the other.

"To see what the unconscious knows, you must accept that the conscious you does not know what it does not know. You do this by not letting what you think you know get in the way of what there is to know. This will place you between the known and unknown, the conscious and unconscious, and allow you to be open to discovery."

There he goes with all that "knowing" stuff. Why does he have to speak in riddles? mumbled Adam to himself, becoming more and more exasperated.

"Let me be clearer."

"Please!"

"Shadows can be your fears, disgust, rejections, feelings of abandonment, prejudices, judgments, repressions of memories, biases, negative thoughts, and all your personal madness that can then be projected onto others that you meet or onto objects and events.

"Here, I will give you a freebie. You exhibit a not-too-well-repressed 'poor me' worldview regarding your experience with family and girlfriends. Many of your actions and points of view are colored by that shadow aspect that you keep pushed into the corners of your unseen self. One of those ways is through a lack of trust; another is through timidity."

"Timidity?" Adam expressed a little more forcibly than he meant to, and then he retreated.

"See? It is the timidness you express toward the barista, the questioning of your value and power to get into a much-wanted relationship. You project onto her the shadow created by the decisions you made about yourself and your experiences."

"Yeah, I've been pretty good at making bad decisions," quipped Adam.

Even though it looked like the magus was ignoring Adam's quips, especially when they expressed suppressed negative energy, he tried to redirect this energy toward something more useful.

"This timidness also suggests that you have suppressed some of your yang power."

"My what?"

"Your yang power, the power of your masculine aspect. In this case, it may be a toning down of your assertive, self-assured, and decisive aspects. This is not surprising, in that you have no real experience of the male model in your life, and what you have had might look weak and less powerful than the female, or yin, energy.

"A yang weakness might affect one's decisiveness, self-assurances, convictions, assertiveness, and ability to discriminate effectively. The absence of or dominance of these yang qualities in either the male or female can limit the effectiveness of one's interactions with the world and thus their access to magic. When one or the other of these yin–yang or feminine–masculine aspects, whether positive or negative in action, dominates, it tends to bias one's ability to perform magic."

"You've used the words 'positive or negative' when talking about the yin and yang energies. What do you mean by 'negative'?"

"Good question! A negative yang energy expressed by either a man or a woman might be aggressiveness versus assertiveness, or timidity rather than assertiveness, or rigidness and inflexibility instead of decisiveness; or it could mean never stopping to reflect because you are too engaged in your need for action or doingness. For the male, the negative aspect to being physically expressive could look like violence.

"The negative feminine, or yin, personality aspects might look like indecisiveness due to being too contemplative or being submissive because of too much receptivity. The positive yin energy might look like being receptive, compassionate, inclusive, and perhaps intuitive."

"Well, I'm all that, at least part of the time."

"Of course, you are! We all have yin and yang qualities to our personality. It is about choosing the quality to express that is appropriate to the moment."

All this caused Adam to pause listening and reflect. He could see portions of himself in all of what the magus was saying. But he hadn't thought of the effects of there having been no father in his life, what with his having had in his life only women and mothers—and those being none too competent, loving, or trustworthy. He would have to think on this some more. He then returned his attention to the old wizard.

"No doubt you see some of yourself in all this. And your actions and expressions of them are probably not consistent across all your dealings with reality. This may be due to the lack of integration of these various parts. But for now, just be aware that you can see yourself, your shadows, your madness, and your level of enlightenment through what you see in or project onto others."

"But I also see the barista as good, kind, smart, and beautiful!" exclaimed Adam, still trying to get traction on this concept.

"Even the goodness in others can point to that unconscious aspect in yourself. What is inside is inextricably connected to what is outside in a very profound way. The truth, Adam, is that your perception of me and everyone else reflects yourself—even the hidden parts of yourself. The fact that you are here at all is a function of the greater wisdom of your bigger self knowing that you needed the nurturance of the positive yin and yang energy that has been missing in your life.

"Your judgments of others and what you think they may have done to you, or the meaning you have assigned to their actions, is what separates them from you and separates you from yourself. When you do this, it cuts you off from your real self—the spirit that you are."

"From myself?" he asked. He then whispered to himself, "How is it that every damn thing seems to come back to me?"

"Yes, we humans use the same judgments on ourselves that essentially separate us from our true selves. We also use our judgments of others to make ourselves seem better than our lesser selves, which we may feel shame for and try to hide. In a way, this is a sin against our real selves. In short, their sin is your sin even though it may look different than yours."

"Sin!" Adam almost spit the word out as though it had a foul taste. "You're not a Holy Roller are you, condemning everyone for his or her transgressions?"

"Not at all! I use the original meaning of the word as used by my friends the Greeks. It meant 'To be separated from the experience of the Creator.' It means 'To miss the mark,' with the mark being that of being one with the creator. Even your judgment and avoidance of the word disconnects you. Again, you react out of your corrupted mind, and this becomes an obstacle to expressing magic. What about the word troubles you so?"

At this Adam felt anger—not fear, nor hurt. What he felt at the deepest level was shame, as though what had happened to him was his fault and his suffering had been justifiable punishment for his sins. It was these feelings that he then confessed to his mentor, who listened carefully.

"Perhaps it has been this you have been hiding from all these years? But how real is your being the cause of your early suffering? How wrong was your reaction to it? Could you have reacted any other way than the way you did when you did?"

"My reaction seems normal when you put it that way."

"Who was responsible for your well-being at your early age?"

"My family, I guess."

"Exactly! At that age, you did not have the tools, experience, or wisdom to take full care of yourself. Taking responsibility for what you have done or not done is laudable and says much for your integrity but taking responsibility for what is not yours is harmful to you and to the greater whole. It is what separates you from others and makes you blind to the magic that resides in others. It is an unconscious myopia that makes you unable to see who you really are.

"When not separated from the rest of reality, you become all of it—what is labeled good and what is labeled bad. When you are consciously or unconsciously separated, it creates a turbulence around and within the soul. In this way, the turbulent winds out there in the world that buffet you are the winds of separation generated from within you. They are all relative to you."

For a moment, the boy could almost feel the gusts of wind trying to knock him off the path and tear him from his goal.

Lead and Gold and the Alchemical Tension between Opposites

"You speak again of good and bad, but this time you speak as though they were relative and not fixed. Are there things and acts that are definitely one or the other?" asked the boy earnestly.

The magus reflected on his answer for a moment before settling on a method that had been used with him when he was a neophyte so very many years earlier.

"Is there not some good that can come from a bad, and a bad that can from a good? Are not each capable of producing the other? Cannot your definition of a good also be another's definition of a bad? Have you not known good people to do bad things for good reasons? Have you heard of doing something bad for the greater good? The pressure to be both exists in all of us, and it is our struggle with it that can bring light from the darkness."

"Yes, I've heard of the ideas of which you speak, magus," he declared with just a hint of combativeness, as though standing ready to defend all that he thought of as good. He imagined that if he lost the benchmark of what was good, he would lose himself as well as the ground he would be able to stand on to live his life with any meaning.

"I know that no thing and no one is perfect, and that sometimes we make errors as to what is good or bad, but I cannot believe that it is all relative. There must be some things that are inherently good and those that are inherently bad."

"These ideas are concepts from the mix of light and dark that exists in all things. Though at times appropriate for the objective world, would not an inflexible weighting of what is or is not good or bad for any situation or circumstance be appropriate for the expression of the magical?

"Rigid definitions for all circumstances may limit your ability to see and do magic; they may even restrict your ability to see what is and is not good or bad. We cannot know precisely what is good or bad. This is the torment of the ethical struggle, but sometimes people need the freedom to be both if the circumstances warrant. Adherence to one definition of either can limit that freedom to give justice to the moment—that is, to act beyond the laws or rules if the situation warrants it. But this requires self-knowledge—that is, the knowledge of where you are whole and where you are not.

"This is not to say that there are no evil acts, because humans who know they are causing harm and do it anyway for no good reason or just for their own personal gain may be doing evil. But it is a struggle within each of us that we must engage with, and we can give proper justice to that struggle only if we know what is within our darker selves that is involved.

"Can we just say for now that anything that separates us from our greater self and from that which created us is bad and that which brings us together toward a greater wholeness is probably good? In addition, can we also say that we cannot know for sure where we stand at any given moment, because of the many gray areas that do not lend themselves to hard and fast definitions? The job of a magician is not to allow oneself to be overwhelmed by the contradiction between the two."

Because he was not yet ready to give ground on the field of this battle, the boy answered reluctantly, "I can live with that for now. But this whole discussion seems a little like madness! But you accuse me of madness. How so?"

"Have you not acknowledged your own madness even in the rejection of it? The madness that resides in all of us is also our guide down the path toward the light. Your attempt to impose comprehensibility on everything is madness itself and closes you off to magic. Have you not noticed that no matter how hard you try to make life understandable, it will not yield its incomprehensibility? Life is crazy; accept it!"

The boy's mind was whirling almost out of control. As a means of distracting and regaining some semblance of control, he noted that the old man was still holding the green book. In his fatigue and confusion, he couldn't contain his building curiosity and asked what the book was about. "Can I see it?" he added, whereupon the old wizard passed him the book with a caveat.

"Look if you must, but you will find nothing of any interest."

He took the book offered, noting his excitement and anticipation of what lay within this mysterious tome, and after running his hand reverently across its face, he opened it only to find that there was no writing in the book. No matter how many pages he turned, all were blank.

"This is crazy! I don't understand," cried the boy incredulously.

"Of course, you do not. Seeing what is there, is not a function of your need to find meaning and understanding but of being open to what is actually there. You cannot see it because you still cling to what you want to see, and that is colored by past decisions and ignored issues. You keep playing the same old themes in your life with the same old outcomes, and this clouds your vision."

"I can see that, and I would really like to let go of all that past stuff—or at least to accept it without letting it determine how I react. It's frustrating and robs me of more than just my vision."

"I hope you will see someday, my boy, and in the seeing be able to choose different outcomes, but we have much yet to do before this day is done," he offered as he took back the book and placed it again on the side table between the chairs.

As the day wore on into the late evening, the lessons were looked at over and over and in great detail, with no question left unturned, until both the magus and the young man, looking somewhat gray, fell back exhausted into their chairs.

"My brain is like mush," sighed the boy.

"Mine as well. Shall we press on or call it a night?"

"I know that time grows short, but I think I need to sleep on what I've heard and process it at a deeper level."

"This is good," exclaimed the magus. "Trusting your inner guide and emerging gnosis during the dreaming will be very helpful. Have a good night, my boy."

The young man got up feeling every joint in his body painfully creaking and shuffled off to his room while the old magus sat before the fire and let go of himself while sighing, "I hope he is going to make it." Then he sat as though waiting for some response.

As he sat and focused upon the fire, a soft glow enveloped him and swirled about, entering his head briefly through the space just above his nose and between his eyes; it traveled down into his heart and then blew out in one slow breath of air. The glow that had entered him had turned dark as it exited his mouth and swirled high into the ceiling. As it did so, his color once again transformed from a dusky gray at the end of a long and tiring day into what could only be called a golden aura. Fully refreshed from his meditation, the magus grasped the arms of the chair and nimbly pushed himself up, donned his jacket, and went out into the night for a brisk walk.

CHAPTER 6

The Source: The Ultima Materia and the Stone of the Philosophers

For nature, as we know, is at once within and without us. Art is the mirror at the interface. So too is ritual, so also myth. These, too, bring out 'the grand lines of nature,' and in doing so, re-establish us in our own deep truth, which is one with that of all being."

—Joseph Campbell, from
The Inner Reaches of Outer Space

The next morning, after a hearty breakfast of fresh fruit and steamed oats, the young student and his mentor took their coffee mugs to the chairs that sat before the familiar fireplace at the other end of the flat and began their study. A light rain had moved into the city, and the warmth of the drink, fire, and friendship brought them both great comfort and the energy to continue the difficult task from the day before.

"So, what of your dreams?" asked the older man, and the younger shared a dream about dark, shadowy figures of people and animals that he was either running from or trying valiantly to kill. He also shared snippets of what seemed to be alchemical poetry—no surprise given what he had already been through.

"These are probably representative of your shadow self—the darker sides of your personality. Running from and trying to kill them off are two sides of the instinctual coin that runs us all. The first is an avoidance metaphor, or what we call the 'flight' instinct, while the latter is the 'fight' instinct—a means of ridding oneself of one's demons. Both are resistance or avoidance symbols to what is and are representative of the ego-self. Knowing when the instinct arises and when to give one or the other its freedom to act or to not act will open one to responding through the power of magic. This allows the spirit self, the bigger self, to have a say. Fundamentally, what you resist will resist you in equal measure."

"By 'spirit-self' do you mean 'soul'?"

"Not exactly. It is of us and will not live beyond the body. The soul is oriented toward everyday life and is the archetype of life and living. It resides in the pits and valleys of life. Basically, it is in the grind that we call life, with all its messiness and illusions. It is always and only communicated through love and is the imaginative potential of our very nature.

"Soul has been said to be a function of morality as well. It is the seer and revealer of truth and meaning, though it is the ego—that part of us that culture, parents, and the personal psyche says we are—that claims this talent for its own. But the ego does not know truth, though it can be the container of it. It only knows itself. As souls, we are wiser than we think we are. As egos, we know nothing. The ego is hard and thus resists magic. One must learn to soften the ego to work with magic.

"The transformation from hard to soft happens when we yield and do not resist, when we bend and are not rigid, and when we are able to use our feelings instead of being used by them; then life becomes more magical. This is the message of the soul.

"On the other hand, spirit is that nonlocal part of us that is not really a part of us, that lives outside the body and is kind of a cosmic body, if you will. It is constantly searching for higher meaning and is the part that seeks to transcend the mess that we humans find ourselves in. It is symbolized by the sun, to which the soul is always drawn, whereas the soul is symbolized by the moon.

"Spirit is beyond what we can intellectually understand and is not earthbound; that is, it is not body bound like the soul. It is what brought you to my door in the first place. It is the intermediary of the source of all things that desires to know itself and realize that desire through the creation of our consciousness.

"You might think of it this way: the spirit is like the ocean, and our souls and the bodies they live through are like waves on that ocean. The wave does not last very long, no more than a few seconds at best, but when it dies it returns to the vast waters of the ocean that created it."

At this Adam smiled, for he knew it was true.

"It is the enlightened or softened ego you that can act as a connector between the two. In many ways, you are soul, and soul is what you experience the world through. The soul can be seen in poetry, music, writing, and acting, or in what we feel and experience as we walk through a quiet forest."

Wholeness: The *Coniunctio*

"The conjunction that is about to happen is the moment when both soul and spirit come together to release a transcendent being. But this can only happen when the shadow-self has been given the light of day, for it is only when introduced into consciousness that the unconscious shadow material can be dealt with. Without the light made available to you through the twelve laws, the shadow will darken your efforts toward wholeness, fullness, and completion.

"And that brings us to the eighth law of magic, which says that one needs to 'call out' their shadows and demons—to name them rather than suppress them. Just because you have negative aspects to your personality does not mean that you are your negative aspects."

"Tell me more."

"Everything in the universe is energy in one form or another, such as your thoughts, your body, your feelings, your resistances or acceptances to what is or is not, and the environment around you. You will also notice that for every positive occurrence, circumstance, situation, feeling, or thought there is an equal and opposite negative. The earth thrives in opposition; each gives energy to the other. Simply put, 'good' only exists in contrast to 'bad,' and vice versa. Resisting the 'bad' only gives it more than its equal share of energy. One needs to learn to bring both sides of oneself into balance without one dominating the other, and one can only do that if one is willing to work openly with one's darker aspects and not suppress them."

"Are life and death also like these conflicting opposites of which you speak?"

"Opposites, as they are often imagined, are not necessarily in conflict with each other. They create each other. You might imagine that life and death are in conflict if you were conditioned to believe that one was a beginning and another an end, or that one was creative while the other was destructive. But what if both are beginnings? What if they both are creative and destructive? You see, both are transitional, with each inextricably bound to the other. They are both at the heart of creation."

Before the magus could continue, the young man, ever impatient, attempted to interrupt yet again. "How do you—"

The magus shot him a warning glance that brought Adam up short. He knew not to interrupt, but he still hadn't learned to rein in his impatience. He bit his tongue and gave his mentor a look and a nod that signaled that he was ready to listen.

The magus went on as though the outburst had been barely noticed. "As I was going to say, you bring the contrasting sides of yourself into balance by not resisting what is, by accepting both sides of yourself, and by working harmoniously with the energy of each.

"By resisting the negative effects of the shadow, these darker aspects will persist. You cannot get rid of the shadow by ignoring, denying, or burying it, because it will then infect everything you do or say.

"Have you ever noticed how some negative aspects or events in your life keep showing up again and again even though you have denied them the energy to exist by refusing to give in to them? Your shadow energy will continue to plague you if you keep it hidden in the dark and deny it access to the light. It is only when you shine a light upon it that it can be dealt with appropriately and effectively. You cannot get rid of the shadow; it is part of you. But you can learn to work with it and then apply its energy constructively. The truth is that you cannot truly see the light without first facing the dark, and in that you will be set free."

Adam was not too comfortable with the idea of facing his hidden demons; after all, he had worked hard to bring them under control—or so he thought.

"You must beware, because there are creatures hidden all around and deep within the dark caverns of your mind, waiting for and causing you to stumble. You must learn to recognize them when they appear or suffer the consequences."

"What do they look like?" asked the boy anxiously.

"They will look like fear, anger, hate, greed, prejudice, arrogance, guilt, depression, and self-criticism. All these creatures that inhabit your dark side. They are not you unless you identify them as such by acting them out or pushing them deep into the corners of your unconscious mind. These dragons of the mind refuse to stay hidden in their caves. They are, as I said, a part of you, but once you discover who you really are, they will become easier to recognize.

"The next, or ninth, law states that magic cannot come from thinking. One needs to quiet the mind and stop thinking things to death. Learn to put your thoughts to sleep. Learn to be still but then pay attention to everything going on around you without labeling what it is.

"We will practice this later through some mindful meditative training— what is known as awareness without thought, pure contemplation, direct perception, or divine nothingness, where you will purposefully focus your attention, observe, and breathe what is happening around and within you without adding your thoughts to it. It is a discipline where you experience what is right in front of you without distorting it with material from the past or seeking to name it or understand it. Just being with something opens you to the beauty of its magic.

"Thinking is actually an impediment to magic. It objectifies the world and thus limits it. Your thoughts are irrelevant to magic anyway. They are just thoughts. This training will also increase your capacity to experience life physically and emotionally more clearly without the human tendency to evade what it does not like. All too often, our thoughts take us away from the space where our vital energies can be accessed.

"When fully attending without entertaining your thoughts, everything can become a revelation, and it is in this place that one becomes one, and all that is left is the magic."

Adam looked then as though he wanted to protest, but the magus cut him off. "What, you believe your thoughts mean something? Well, as they say, do not believe everything you think. Magic does not care what you think. Learn to let go of your thoughts and you will make room for magic.

"By 'let go of your thoughts' I do not mean for you to resist your thoughts; nor do I mean for you to add your subjective projections to them either—that is, do not judge them, but do not reject the judgements either. Many of your thoughts come from others and thus color your personal experience, making it hard to own your observations. Accept them all as a part of you without becoming attached to them. In fact, the process of letting go that I have been sharing opens the door and allows you to fall into the magic.

"In the tenth law, it is stated that magic does not come from the rational. Live at least some of your life in the incomprehensible and trust your intuitive self. This ties in nicely with the 'thinking' part of the ninth law. Thinking is of the rational self. It is necessary in very many ways, but it cannot be used to summon forth and manifest the power of magic.

"It is your intuitive self that you must learn to strengthen, trust, and engage without dressing it up with logical proofs that are only used to rationalize the intuitive experience to make it seem credible. Intuition is not rational, and yet it can lead you to the truth, the truth of yourself, and it is there that you will find the magic. It is there that the magic will find you.

"Intuition is being able to look within with the third eye, that place between and above your eyes, to find the balance that is needed in any moment and to see clearly what is truly real—what is truly there beyond the ordinary senses. It is not the result of ordinary deduction or scientific inference or even physical experience. It is of the extraordinary and is often perceived as being mystical in nature. Some say that the third eye intuition is an unconscious aspect that opens one to the magical possibilities of life and gives one reality. It is also where one can 'feel' the sound of the universe.

"It is said by the ancients that the third eye is an energy center where we transcend the duality that is our either/or, or cause/effect, perception by freeing us from our time-bound reality and releasing us into what some might call a super-reality. It is one of the connections to wisdom and insight and an extra sense that some call the sixth sense. It is also where the mother of the Universe can be heard in the sound of Om."

"I've heard of this third eye, but how does one access it?"

"Strengthening your inner eye is the first step. Most people are so caught up in trying to logically reason out the world that they have left their inner wisdom, their intuitive selves, in a weakened state.

"Along with this intuitive sense, there is also the phenomenon of noncausal events, or synchronicities, which will point you toward other realities or new perceptions. As with intuition, being open to what seem to be coincidences can bring you knowledge of what is normally not seen."

"Do you mean that there are events or effects that have no cause? How's that possible?"

"When events that seem to be connected and yet are not, such as when you are thinking of someone that you have not thought of in years and that person suddenly calls you on the phone. Another example might be when you are feeling down and wish or pray for a change, and then someone compliments you for something you thought no one had any idea you had done, without any solicitation on your part other than the silent wish or prayer."

"I recall a time when I was being so harshly judgmental of myself that my self-esteem tanked, when suddenly a car drove past me with a vanity license plate that said, 'BE SILENT.' And the voice in my head quieted."

"Yes! It is just like that. That was the universe aligning itself with your need. The effect is part of the magic I have been talking about. These synchronicities can signal your need to take a different direction in the moment or in your life."

Dreams as the Alchemical Vitriol that Dissolves the Barriers to the Inner Self

"They can also announce that you are exactly where you need to be. These are seeming coincidences that take on more meaning when you realize that the universe is always talking to you."

"I was taught that there were only five senses, but you've brought up seven so far. Are there more?"

"There are! There is a sense of where your body is in space and time, electromagnetic field sensitivity at a cellular level, the sense of the nous, or the spirit sense, which can predispose one to mystical experiences and insights, precognition or premonition, inner knowing or illumination, and the simple ability to detect when someone is looking at you. These are just a few of the senses that are subliminal sensory systems."

"What do you mean about inner knowing or illumination? I don't get it."

"It's an instantaneous knowing of something without there being evidence. It is kind of an instinctual knowing or a silent knowing. It is a way of silencing the mind so that one can hear, see, and feel the energy of places outside the restrictions of the cognitive system. You practiced a part of it when you allowed your mind to quiet by not entertaining the voice in your head. It is also that peaceful feeling at the end of the centering prayer you practiced. Remember?"

"I do!" Just the memory of these moments brought a sense of peace and knowing to Adam.

"Through practice, these senses that we all have can be consciously activated to provide more data regarding our surroundings, both inner and outer.

"Dreamwork is another way to see or hear what the world is saying and can also help to strengthen the third eye. Learning to be more silent through routine meditation can also help you to access and communicate with reality in a deeper and broader way.

"Dreams are one of the four states of consciousness, along with wakefulness, sleeping, and awareness without thought. I will have to get you a journal for all those dreams of yours. They are important and can provide you access to your inner gnosis and wisdom, as well as the material you have buried to not have to deal with it. Dreams reveal one's true nature and the true nature of the world around oneself.

"The truth is that you cannot really see the world through just your conscious mind. The material hidden within your unconscious and the material of the collective images of mankind can add immeasurable understanding and awareness. In fact, most of your available wisdom is hidden in the unconscious mind. Learning to 'read' your dreams can open the door to that wisdom. I will teach you how to do this by redirecting the energy you use on your dreams and how the energy you use on maintaining other aspects of your current level of psyche development gets in the way of seeing the magic all about you."

"Isn't dreaming just another form of one's imagination?"

"You act as though the imaginal is of no importance in that it is not real. The imaginal world of one's dreams offers clues that there is something beyond the limited ego-self and its culturally imposed boundaries and that one needs to cast off into realities' unknowns to really see what is possible. The truth is that imagination is what stimulates reality and its creation.

"I, for one, will stand in a forest and listen for all the sounds and breathe in all the smells, reach out to feel the textures of the plants, the soil, and wind—all that which opens the heart to the magic. The whole planet literally hums with the creative energy of magic, and when you align with that energy, it becomes thou."

At this Adam felt a stimulating chill thrilling at the nape of his neck. Shivering briefly, he shook it off and refocused on the magus.

"You will also need to hone your attentional and observational skills. Try observing before figuring out. Sometimes seeing through the inner eye can help you to see more than the physical eye ever will. A well-developed third eye can out figure the best, most reasoned, and most knowledgeable thought. I also tune into my spirit guides. They are always there, waiting to help."

"Spirit guides?"

"Yes. Sometimes they will come to you in dreams as a deceased parent or grandparent, a teacher, or an angel or animal. Sometimes they are just soft voices from the depths of your being. Often, they show up in times of stress and can just barely be heard above the chaotic din of your constantly chattering mind or the inane wordiness of the everyday world, but hear them you must, for they are there to guide you through the maelstrom and sometimes even to push you into it."

This seemed a bit ominous to the boy, and he wondered aloud, "How will I know these guides?"

"You will know them in good time, my boy," asserted the magus, looking into the distance as though he were looking into the future. "But let us get back to the third eye and your question about access. To access, I begin with mindful breathing and then visualize a blue or purple ball that often will activate the inner eye and open me to the real world—the world where magic lies.

"Look at something without knowing or giving it a name; follow your sense of it without expectation, belief, or definition; and experiment with what you see. Observe its reaction, then follow your sense of it and let it guide you. Just be in the mystery of all things without the constraint of thinking you know.

"Basically, just embrace not knowing and see what you get. Knowing fills the mind and crowds out the empty spaces where the spirit dwells. Walk outside in the early morning to greet the rising sun, and with your eyes closed, listen to and feel the world around you. Do this without labeling the experiences. How are we doing so far?"

"Good, good, keep going," encouraged the young man as he motioned his mentor to continue and gently placed his cup upon the side table between the two chairs.

"The eleventh law states that magic grows from the secret orderliness of chaos."

At this Adam screwed up his face in confusion.

"No, really!" cried the magus. "There is a beauty in the unpredictable. Contrary to what you have been taught and now believe, life is not deterministic. As I have said before, humans have an odd sense of time. In truth, cause is not always prior to effect. Our brains have been conditioned to think that everything follows a linear pattern where time only flows in one direction. But it only seems thus because time is happening at, well, all the same time. Once you can fully grasp that, you will see that past/future and cause/effect are no longer obstacles to your travel through them. Whenever you want to be, you are already there!

"The world operates in patterns, and the balance that all systems seem to strive for does not always follow a set or deterministic pattern. Nothing in your so-called reality can be accurately determined. Though situations can look remarkably similar even down to their minute constituencies, they are not. In short, small differences within virtually similar patterns can make huge differences and radically change your perceived reality. Uncertainty rules the world, young man. So, allow yourself to be confused and uncertain. Within that uncertainty is a pattern to be discerned, but it is not to be discerned through the rational mind, as I said earlier with the tenth law.

"Ultimately, thinking that you know something about what is real can be very limiting to living or seeing what is real, to perceiving what is real, and to performing real magic. To think that you know something produces an expectation—the expectation that the universe will always support that knowledge. But that is not how it really works, is it? And when the universe lets you down, you get upset, right?"

Adam nodded and the magus went on.

"This is because you think that you are in control when you are not at all, and you never have been. I might also add that before you clear out the junk you have buried in your unconscious mind, you have never been at choice with anything, and that so-called free will of yours requires the ability to be at choice—that is real choice." Here he emphasized the word "real."

"Real choice is affected by your expectations and by your beliefs. These are your prejudices, which also repress the expression of magic as well as your psychic life. They are part of your inner dialogue, which affects what you see, how you feel, and how you live your life."

"Real choice?"

"Yes. If you cannot say both no *and* yes to everything, then you are not really at choice. You have to be okay with either state of being. What you can then do is 'choose' what is best for the situation and circumstance you find yourself in; that is the choice to conform or not to conform, based on what is necessary in the moment—what is best for you and everyone and everything around you.

"You also cannot be consciously at choice if the material is not dealt with in your unconscious mind—you know, all the stuff you have hidden there: all the instinctual stuff, all the cultural stuff, and the stuff that Mommy and Daddy put into your head that is actually running the show. Being clear about your hidden motivations is a prerequisite for free will, which is, of course, a requisite for magic. These expectations are what keep us shackled to the mundane and limited in our ability to be magic.

"The final part of the choice equation is to act and take what you get. Resistance to what is will only keep your decision stuck and closed off to other possibilities.

"In the twelfth law, one is told that one must maintain one's authority over expectations and standards by remaining at choice with one's behaviors, thoughts, and self-expressions.

"You may have the thought that if you could just change your thoughts, this could change who you are being. The 'positive thinking' gurus want you to learn to have positive thoughts to deal with your negative thoughts. But all this does is mask your negative thoughts. They are still there and still informing your reality, and as such they also mask the magic that is available in just being who you are.

"In short, young man, be what you are, not what you think you ought to be, and certainly not what someone else wants you to be or think or believe, even if that someone else is me. Let go of what you think you are or are afraid you are or do not want to be to become who you really are. Stop trying to fit into what is not you." The magus then paused for effect.

"If these laws do not resonate, then do not follow them. You cannot follow them anyway, because you would then be violating the resistance caution of the eighth law in that you would be resisting that which you know to be wrong for you by trying to force them to be right. This, as you now know, only gives energy to the power of opposition that will work against you."

"Eh? I don't get it. You're negating all you've said. Are you telling me that you don't believe in what you've been saying?"

"Of course, I do not have to believe—because I *know*. Belief is malleable, an opinion, though people act as though it is fixed, but nothing is fixed, and knowing is neither fixed nor malleable is experiential.

"The 'knowing' that I have been talking about all these days is the knowing that comes from wholeness. It is when the intuitive becomes embodied in us and manifests through our experiences that we can illustrate the truth of the knowing.

"But truth itself is not an absolute. Today I experience something that seems to be true, but if I then act as if it is always true, I blind myself to what is true tomorrow. Truth cannot sit forever in a box because it is always a moving target that brings light to the moment."

"So, there're no absolutes?"

"Absolutely!" declared the old wizard with a broad grin. "But if you act as though that is an absolute, then you will be caught in a belief and be forever in an imaginary and never-ending loop."

"That loop seems very real at the moment," cried Adam in frustration.

"All truths are just hypotheses. If you take these laws I have shared with you and expect or believe them to do the magic, then you will be sorely disappointed. The laws are only a framework or matrix to live within. The real importance of believing versus knowing is not in the knowing but in the understanding of what you know and then letting go of what you know to see the reality—that is, to perceive reality directly without the encumbrances I have been talking about.

"Adam, I hope that you can now see the secret to magic is that you are as magic as you wish to be. The reality that you know is a function of your desire to know it. This you have done, or you could not have gotten as far as you have in your search for magic.

"As you are now aware, the real secret to magic cannot be found in that part of you that knows or believes it can only be found within the source of your very being. It is only by surrendering what you think you are and what you think you know to that source that magic can come forth. All the rest is just a 'do,' but the source is a something and a being *and* an immeasurable and indescribable nothing that you connect to in order to be magic.

"Connect to the source and you will *be* the magic. Live your life in the source and there is no end to what you are."

"What is this source?" pleaded the young man.

"Ah, yes, the question that defines the essence of the spiritual quest. This is what you must wrestle with over the next day and night. I could name it, but this would be meaningless without the experience of it. You are about to experience what the ancients called a 'quickening'—that is, an experience of spiritual awakening and a place of healing where your separated self becomes whole again. Sometime during the night, you will be transported to a sacred place, a place of the large stone and the well of the mother, where you will witness the coming of the two into one.

"I suggest that you go be with yourself and take all that I have taught, all that I have said, all that I have alluded to, and all that you have experienced here and meditate on it. Find your own knowing. Tap into the imaginal of your being and open to the wordless mystery of it.

"You may even want to embody some of it, and by that, I mean to bring it to life and dialogue with it as though it were alive within you. I will give you one hint, however: the answer is not in the head or in the words you use to try to describe it. The answer, like so many other answers, will probably come when you are at a loss for words. The knowing of which I speak comes without words."

The old wizard then waved his palm across the face of the green book, and a stone appeared that he then picked up and handed to Adam. It was a curious object in that it felt both cold and warm, and painted upon its face was a circle divided into four colors—red, yellow, black, and white—with a cross inscribed where the colors met. Adam looked up from the stone with a quizzical look.

"It is a quaternity, a talisman of wholeness. It will help you keep your bearings. Keep it with you."

"It's just a rock. What good will it do?"

"Never underestimate the power of four, Adam."

Adam cocked his head to the side as though trying to divine the magus's meaning, shrugged, and then tossed the stone into the air, flipping it end over end like a coin, and caught it, getting a measure of its heft. He then put it in his pocket. It felt reassuring. He wasn't sure what the power of four was all about, but he could ask about that later. Right now, the magus wanted him to have it, so that would just have to do.

"Remember that finding the source has to be done before the joining of the moon and sun two days from now, for if you do not succeed, you will be trapped between and behind them forever."

Never had he felt so alone and with so much riding on his ability to navigate something for which he had no map to guide him.

Sensing his disturbance, the magus presented him with a parting gift.

The Four Psychopomps

"You will be met by a number of transformative rebirths throughout this night that can, if you have learned well, free you from your endless cycle of death and rebirth, but you will not be alone in this journey.

"As you wander before the eclipse, be open to the voice of the telluric mother, Aerial rising up from the earth through you. She will guide and protect you through the conjoining and into your rebirths. She will be the midwife to your reawakening. She is an ancient energy, the hub of the universe that will lead you through your personal Armageddon. Listen to her, for she knows the way.

"You will also be met by three spirit animals upon your journey through the darkness: the eagle, owl, and raven. Coepio, the eagle, will announce the beginning of this trial and give you the strength to endure; Focus, the owl, will bring your attention to the great change and will aid you in vision and intention; and Rebis, the raven, will announce the end and its celebration of transformation. There is also the energy of your own soul and spirit to keep you company and to protect you, but they will not reveal themselves until you have delt with your darker aspects, which only you have the power to deal with. Heed the four but be open to your soul and spirit as well, for they are your wisdom guides for the transition."

"An eagle, here in the city?" mused Adam aloud.

With no response forthcoming, the young man shrugged, picked up his jacket, and went out into the morning drizzle, heading almost aimlessly toward the city forest at the end of the street, but doing so with an air of what could only be called intention.

CHAPTER 7

The Alchemical Sacred Marriage: The Unus Mundus

… my mind was flooded with an intuitive knowing that everything is interconnected—that this magnificent universe is a harmonious, directed, purposeful whole. And that we humans, both as individuals and as a species, are an integral part of the ongoing process of creation.

—Edgar Mitchell, Apollo 14 astronaut

Adam wandered seemingly undirected for what seemed hours up the hill and through several neighborhoods. Meanwhile, great mountainous clouds were building above the headlands and beginning to menace the city. Night was creeping across the landscape. Eventually he made his way off the street and down a shallow embankment that ended near a lamppost casting a rather sickly glow that barely illuminated the ground directly beneath it, let alone the path it stood beside.

At the end of the path and just beyond a little meadow, he stood at the edge of a rather ill-kempt city forest. He looked around him but could barely make out the anemic glow of the lamppost in the distance, which was now shrouded in the mist that seemed to roll in from every corner, bush, and crevice, giving the landscape a cold, foreboding feel.

As he made his way into the ever-thickening forest, he found himself along an unfamiliar and poorly kept path that was much less worn than the first but was covered by rock and root waiting to trip him up. Cautiously he walked into the mist, where large drops of water slid from the trees and splashed against his face and ran down his neck and into the fabric of the shirt, which was now clinging fast to his body.

He almost didn't notice, for his mind was taken up with other things— things like thoughts about something called "source" and "intention" and about his potentially not being ready to transform before the moon and sun conjoined. *What does it mean to be stuck behind and between the sun and the moon?* Whatever it meant, it didn't feel as though it were a good thing. And who was this mother he was to be on the lookout for?

Rain began to fall, and he could vaguely smell a pleasant, earthy odor of leaves mixed with the dampened soil and grasses. In the distance, he saw a flash, and thunder rumbled raucously across the city. "The dragons of the East and West are duking it out," he whispered to himself. As he stood there mesmerized by the movement of the storm, he had a vision of two dragons. He could see their long and sinewy bodies—the male without wings and the female with her wide feathery pinions soaring and clashing among the clouds. They seemed to be fighting over the dark moon held by the female dragon, who had flown in from the southeast over the mountains.

This was the second time a dragon had threatened his well-being, only these dragons brought with them rains and flooding waters instead of fire. However, these dragons could spit electrical fire if they chose. But even water could not put out their fire. These dragons were also just as emotionally laden, but with a different message.

Adam could see that they were youngsters having only recently hatched and grown gargantuan in minutes, but they were dangerous, nonetheless.

What tale did they bring with them? What was it that these warrior daemons had to tell him? Was the moon they were fighting over an omen for the impending confluence and the act of transformative integration that the magus had spoken of? Was the flood they brought with them auguring an emotional overwhelm, or could it be that their rain was the nurturing of a new beginning? As they clashed and sparred with one another, flashes of lightning discharge shattered the air, with both dragons recoiling after every strike and blow.

The storm had come from the northwest across the sea and had rolled over the headlands and then suddenly and ferociously hit the gateway into the bay and rushed through the canyons of tall buildings—the hills and valleys of the city. "How strange," whispered the young man, "that nothing had been predicted." For a moment, his thoughts and fears had been lost in the winds whipping about him, but they soon found him again.

Surely, he could do this; after all, he had a clever mind, did he not? But his thoughts just spiraled into chaos, and he couldn't get them to settle and focus. Fear built up as he realized that he might have missed something important that the old man had given him—something that would mean either light and life or just darkness and death. If he couldn't find it, he could be trapped behind the eclipse forever.

This was like the ultimate final exam, and he feared that maybe he hadn't studied hard enough or long enough to be prepared for the most important test of his life. It reminded him of all those disquieting dreams in which he came to the end of the college term and discovered that he hadn't gone to class. Dare he wing it? Could he avoid the consequences if he failed?

Panic started to settle into his every thought, crept up his spine to his shoulders, and brought up from his churning stomach bile that burned and tasted most sour and foul in his mouth. The fear became a solid thing that began to settle and weigh heavily upon his limbs, slowing his every movement. The fear then sparked another uneasy thought that seemed to hover above his head: *What if I am not properly trained or let that part of his mind that is always trying to be in control move me in a way that leads to failure? It isn't as though this has never happened before. It happens all too often.* He shrugged as though reconciled to his inevitable failure.

He remembered that more often than he liked, his mind's voice would send him in the wrong direction and would blow like the wind through the trees, making him believe that the spooky noises heard were some real demons, when they were nothing more than the creaking of branches rubbing together. But what could he trust if not the voice he had always lived with and followed?

The Primordial Mother as Anima

He reached into his pocket and found the stone talisman the old man had given him earlier, and it felt warm to the touch. He knew that there was no special magic in the stone, but somehow it still brought him some reassurance that all would be right. In this momentary shift in focus, where his thoughts were on something other than himself, he recalled something the old man had taught him, and he refocused his mind on his breathing. *Breathe in, breathe out, breathe in ...* Soon enough the fear began to melt away and he could once again get his bearings.

As he let go, he let out a big sigh, and at that point a softer and incredibly loving thought—no, not a thought, but another voice he hadn't heard before—whispered and sang as though from Circe, the daughter of the sun herself, from behind and below, infusing his very being though almost ignored by the all-too-busy and chattering voice of the ego-mind. But the boy caught it and brought it to consciousness.

As he did so, a barely visible apparition came as though of the air itself and this face, hidden in the breath that gave him life, floated down beside him. She seemed familiar, but he was pretty sure he'd not seen her before, yet ...

Before he could speak, the vision faded.

Quickly he pulled his cell phone from his pocket and tapped it, looking to see how much time he had left before the eclipse. When he looked closer, he found he was looking at his watch. Time was playing tricks on him again even outside the house. He would have to work in the future on staying put in one time stream at a time. But the voice intruded on his thoughts once again: "Your cleverness only separates you from reality," she sang.

Aerial: "… a beautiful ghostly form of a woman who came to him like a vision of an oracle from the ancient world and whose face shimmered just inches from his own.…"

Then another sound intruded into the mental maelstrom, and with it a beautiful ghostly form of a woman who came to him like a vision of an oracle from the ancient world and whose face shimmered just inches from his own. "This is not just about you," she whispered. "Caring only about your own condition will lead only to doom—your doom and the doom of us all. That is the wrong direction to travel. The energy that fuels your ability to produce magic is love and not the self-centeredness of fear." Her voice sounded as though it were coming out of the hollows of the earth and seemed to echo all around him. Was this one of the visions the old man had prophesized?

As the vision faded, Adam stopped walking and turned and looked about him as though trying to find the source of the voice that had so successfully penetrated his fears and quieted the little voice of his own that he had become so used to hearing. He then remembered the magus's advice to trust in this deeper voice. And her song continued.

Once more the vision came to him.

"Stop trying to be so clever. I am here; I have always been here with you, and in you, beyond your thoughts. All your thinking, all your so-called knowledge, will only lead you further astray. There is a way, but it is not through your mind. Let go of it *NOW!*" Her words felt to Adam like a clap of thunder and focused his attention. "There are no answers in the chaotic voice of your head. It knows only itself. You, as well as most people, imagine that you are only what the voice says you are.

"Your wisdom does not lie within the sound of this clever little fellow that you think is the real you—this voice that promises answers or thinks it has the answers. You must reason beyond this voice. You have the power to use this reason, but like so many others you have lost your way because you have forgotten the way. You had it once when you were very young, but it was just too hard to hear over the din of the older ones, and you soon forgot and began to take on their way—the wrong way. It was then that you walked out of the light and into the darkness."

"But how do you do this way of which you speak?" pleaded Adam, forgetting momentarily the law of not doing.

"You cannot 'do' the way or think yourself through it. All that will do is confuse or create the illusion of knowledge. The more ingenious you try to be, the more strange and mysterious things will tend to happen. Be content that there is an order within the chaos but that you cannot find it by searching for it. You find it by not looking for it. Desire of any kind will hide all but the edges of reality."

"But everything is so crazy around me. How can I do this?" pleaded the young man.

"Be simple and be empty. Be at one with the dust of the earth. Do not resist the end, for it is just a beginning. To have only mind is to suffer death; being in touch with, though not bound by, the mother, the source of us all, brings freedom from that.

"Seek not answers from outside the mother. She is the powerful aspect of the feminine and is the key to opening the door to the magic of the world. Your masculine form is what you use to act and assert upon your decision to walk through the door, but it is your feminine aspect that provides you the opening. It is the marriage between the two that will make it possible for you to wield the magic. But as with the masculine aspect, the feminine is of two minds: the dark and the light, the toxic and the empowering.

"Seek your answers from both your mothers: she of the bright light and she of the dark and deadly. One is an illusion, while the other reflects your deeper self, and yet both inform your being. You must confront them both and recognize them for who they really are. In this you will be the way."

"Who is this mother of whom you speak? It cannot be my mother, for I barely knew her. She died when I was only two, and I cannot even remember her face except that in my memories and dreams it always seemed to have a smile.

"The only mother I've ever known was my mother's sister, and she was none too happy to be saddled with me. I was her burden until I turned ten; then she left to go grocery shopping one morning and I never saw her again. How could she do that? I was just a kid! Was it something I did or didn't do?" He choked back the tears that usually came with this memory, and the words caught in his throat. He thought how odd it was that he should confide so readily with this phantasm memories and feelings he hadn't shared with anyone else.

"Oh, there were other mothers, those who got paid to watch over me, until one day after I turned sixteen there was an accident with the last one, and she died—my foster mom, I mean. Both she and her husband were killed in a car wreck, but he and I didn't get along anyway.

"I was alone and decided that I could just take care of myself. So, I avoided child protective services and didn't return to the system. Weeks later, when they realized my foster parents were gone, so was I. They hadn't been able to help all that much anyhow. I had saved up some cash from odd jobs. I bummed a few sofas and a couple of garage stays from friends until I finished school, and I then conned the registrar at the university to give me a scholarship. And the rest, as they say, is history."

The vision was now sitting beside him on a rock beside the path and looking him in the eye with her hand gently on his knee.

"That is truly a sorrowful tale and says more about you—your courage, wit, many tears shed, and stamina—than it does about these women. But the mother of whom I speak is not the one who birthed you and for one moment in time showed the courage to go through the pain necessary to grow something new and magical in your singular being. No, I speak of the mother who is the earth, from which all things grow. She is the feminine counterpart of the masculine sun; she is the moon and the empress of all being and the ruler of the Chthonic realm, or underworld of the unconscious psyche. She is of the life-giving wind that never shows her face and is your entry into the deeper self and the archetypal desire to know the real self. In her there are no secrets. Let her into your conscious being, and she will guide you every step of the way."

"I do not understand this unconscious psyche. What is that?"

"Human beings live in two different worlds simultaneously, the conscious and unconscious, each with its own organizing paradigm. The power of four is what drives us toward wholeness and magic."

"There's that power of four again that the magus talked about," said Adam to himself, and the stone in his pocket seemed to move in sympathy with his thought.

"When we sleep, the consciousness of the waking mind is disengaged, and yet something stimulates the brain into creating a symbolic world that speaks to hidden material that the consciousness of the waking mind does not notice, like what this mind brings up as thoughts and feelings associated with the world it finds itself in.

"To be whole and thus powerful in magic, one needs to be able to access and understand both worlds. There are archetypes or inherited modes of functioning living in both worlds that can help us to navigate the whole. The mother is one of these."

Intuitively he knew that the mother was a spirit guide into the unfamiliar territory that was to lead him into a new way of being and would give him the power to survive the conjunction (i.e., the great synthesis) that was about to take place. But he also knew that he would have to untie the knot that bound him to his birth mother and her surrogates. These were the knots that kept him tied to their memory and all the decisions he had made regarding his lack of trust in them for his well-being. It was now time to let go and open to this new spirit.

"What must I do?"

"Create while not claiming so as to be the way," the voice said. "Give up your mind. Be not of one way or the other but be it all. Let the conflict come to balance in you and you will have found your mother.

"Stop behaving as an adult, for they know nothing but cleverness and knowledge. Let go of your adult knowing until you are empty of all you have learned. You cannot experience your true mother through knowing the ways of the world. Stop doing and just *be* for a moment."

"Be; do not do—I've heard that before." But before he could further engage the spirit, the storm seemed to grow in its rage.

"Be small," cried the voice now barely heard above the din of the storm. "Be small and your greatness will grow. But not the small of the little mind, where you see only yourself. See simplicity in the complex."

"It would be hard not to feel small in a storm such as this," mumbled Adam to himself.

"Listen carefully, Adam. As with an ocean, peace is not to be found on the surface, where all is restless. You need to sink below the surface, where it is quiet, to find it. Find your peacefulness by being at one with your inner conflicts, and you will become a peacemaker, for only the real peacemaker can bring balance and wholeness to either himself or the world.

"Also, you need to lose your self-importance. Self-grandeur or self-importance is illusory and wastes the energy needed to see and be magic. Trying to be first has separated you from everything else, and magic cannot exist in a condition of separation, divisiveness, and self-importance."

"That's exactly what the magus told me!" exclaimed Adam half aloud.

It was as though the old wizard, and this empress mother were connected and somehow aligned.

As he mused on her words, consciousness began to fade, but something new was beginning to grow within him.

Again, he checked his cell and was stunned to find that no time at all had passed since the last time he checked. The whole lengthy dialog between him and the voice had taken no time at all. "How can that be?" he wondered aloud.

In the darkness of the night, he stumbled blindly, unable to make his way through sight alone, depending now upon sound and touch and his inner guide. All around him, he could hear small, plaintive voices mumbling in the wind and slowly becoming shriller, when suddenly there was a great flash of light, and the sky was torn by the ripping sounds of thunder pounding everything about him. The dragons battle had found him in a vulnerable space and though not directed at him threatened to strike him with their bolts of fire.

One more step and his world quivered slightly. The forest seemed to change both in density and feel, as though he had been transported somewhere else—which indeed he had. The park had somehow transformed into a vast expanse of tangled woods at the edge of a valley stretching far into the distance and into the clouded night.

There was a strange otherworldly feel to this place that left Adam even more uneasy. Cautiously he looked about him, feeling as though there were animals here watching his every move and stealthily tracking him to take any advantage he may offer them. He'd heard of wolf packs in wildernesses such a this and wanted to be ready to run if they threatened, though he knew he probably couldn't outrun them. But he thought he might be able to climb a tree to get out of their way if given a head start.

"God, I hope there's nothing out there but my imagination," he pleaded.

Feeling a little light-headed, he reached out a hand to steady himself against a rock wall that had appeared beside him. On closer inspection, the wall was part of a four-sided stone well. *What is a well doing here, in the middle of nowhere?* mused Adam.

He could just see something writhing in the muddy stream along the side of the well. "Snakes!" he cried out. "Oh God, what a nightmare this is turning into!"

Because we all are affected by and affect our environment simultaneously through the energies that we share, Adam noticed that from deep inside the earth something was arising.

Suddenly the great eagle, Coepio, swooped down from his perch on a giant stone dolmen, flapping his wings vigorously and creating a turbulent wind before him, with the rain coming from behind and becoming a maelstrom that was like a ravenous raptor clawing its sharp, cold talons deep into his bones. "Now it really begins," said Adam to himself, recalling the old wizard's prediction, and he readied himself for whatever was next. He could feel the power of the raptor giving him energy but also threatening to take it away.

The Anemoi, gods of the wind, came at him furiously from all four directions, but he stood his ground. He was not, however, ready for the psychic storm raging within his consciousness; it had awakened the evil Windingo, which seemed to come up from the deep well of his unconscious mind to steal his soul. They tore at him, consuming his courage and good sense. He felt the rushed beating of his heart, which thumped in his ears and filled his chest, with each breath becoming a major undertaking.

He instantly despaired of all hope, with the storm blowing him senseless. Everything seemed lost. His suffering seemed unbearable, when just moments before it had seemed nothing could bend him. *What is this dark place?* he asked himself. *Where did it come from?*

For a moment, the voice of reason that had sat with him was drowned out in the downpour. Her vision had disappeared, though he still felt her presence.

The rain had caused two fast-moving rivulets to form on either side of the path, reducing it to a narrow strip of land that he had to carefully negotiate lest he wind up knee-deep in mud and water that in its fury might carry him down into the valley below. It reminded him of the mentor's story of walking the ridge while all about you is trying to knock you down.

He let go of the well wall but had progressed only a half dozen hard-won steps along the ridge when demonic forces and water spirits both inside and out seemed to tear at him, driving him to his knees and washing away all hope that he'd survive the night. Bunyips crawled out of the newly formed rivers, snakes slithered toward him, hungry wolves threatened at the wood's edge, and the cold, screaming winds slashed at his face.

Though he did not understand from where came the next words from his mouth, he found himself invoking the name of the first magus as he cried out an adjuration: "Dear God, the winds of Aurora and Lilith, and anger of Artemis drive me to my knees. See me on my knees. I kneel before you. I kneel; do you not see? I have done you no wrong; a wrong I have done you not, and I bow, bow, bow to your power. May you in your infinite compassion call the Abrasax, the delight of dawn, to lift me instead in my time of need."

Though he held out little hope that his entreaty into the universe would have any magical effect, he knelt there, bowed, muddied, humbled, and feeling defeated, but opened himself to accept whatever was next.

Almost on cue, another mysterious though much more loving wind—a pneuma or spirit breath, if you will—came up from the earth through the stone well and, like a gentle specter, stroked his cheek and lovingly wrapped its arms about him. It was warm and familiar, like a long-passed member of his family still loving and protecting him from beyond the grave. He had always had a special place in his heart for the wind in that it seemed almost alive to him, and he would find himself talking to it as though it could hear and feel his presence. This time it filled him with its energy and gave him hope where moments before there had been none.

"Are you Aerial, the mother whom the magus referred to?" Again, the soft, loving voice of the mother filled his mind.

"I am she and also Gabriella, who will midwife your rebirth."

As with all the magical creatures the magus had alluded to, Adam didn't understand their duality. *How can the mother be both Aerial and Gabriella?*

As though reading his thoughts, the mother answered, "I am also Jophiela and Uriela. I am whomever is needed in the moment. Now remove your shoes and plant your feet upon the altar of the earth. Let her energy rise up through you and fill every cell of your body."

As he was told, he removed his shoes, and feeling the grass and muddied earth between his toes, he absorbed a sense of strange power.

Straightening up, he looked closer at the fearsome creatures that had been tearing at him, and he saw their real faces and recognized them as those darker selves that the wizard had warned him of earlier. They flinched at his gaze, and no longer being able to hide in the light of his recognition, their power was drained, and they vanished.

It was then that a great and elegant stag with deep black eyes appeared alongside a companion mare of pure white with a single horn upon its forehead whose eyes were as blue as the sky. He knew that these powerful creatures were his soul and spirit, still wild but protecting him from the chaos. They could not appear until Adam had confronted the dark creatures. Straightening, he walked slowly forward, flanked by the two new visitors.

The storm endured had been like a Valkyrie that had chosen him on this unlikely battlefield to move into a place of transformation.

The *Aurea Hora* (The Golden Hour)

The storm ended as suddenly as it had begun. The rain and wind had stopped, with only the occasional pitter-patter sound of droplets falling off the ends of tree branches and leaves. The willow thicket, with its narrow leaves and spikey fronds that he had been pushing through, was bent and heavily laden with water, as were the blue gums that seemed even grayer than usual, their bark having been virtually exfoliated during the storm. The pines and firs, too, were bent earthward, with some branches resting upon the ground as though the trees had been trying to hold themselves up and steady their trunks against the wind. Curiously, there were tall, spindly bays bent over and forming what looked like the Gothic ceiling of an ancient cathedral. Only the mighty oak stood tall.

The clouds had begun to clear. Patches of the semidark and velvety blue waning night were turning to a lighter blue that peeked out from the grayness, and the voice that had kept him company through the maelstrom was now gone.

The lights from many eyes peering out from the woodland around him converged into a single stream and entered his body. Sometime during the night and in this now becalmed and darkling wood, he had let go of himself and blended with the surrounding forest.

An owl hooted from somewhere at the woodland's edge as though to augur a change and pass its wisdom. It was then that the boy noticed yet another curious transformation in the world about him and turned his attention toward the sound of the owl. "That must be Focus calling out to me," muttered Adam.

As he stood there looking across another meadow toward the line of trees where he had heard the soulful call of this forest spirit, he scanned the area around himself, absorbing the focused energy of this third spirit guide of his journey, and noted that where he had once ended at the edge of his skin, where all else began, no longer defined his being, and he found himself living everywhere and, in every creature, simultaneously. The white mare nuzzled against his neck, and he reached out to stroke her head and soft flowing mane.

No longer of the finite, he could see—no, not really see, but feel—the infinite and feel the energy of the magic all about him. It was a heady and somewhat disorienting feeling, yet it brought with it a deep peacefulness and sense of belonging—a permanent belonging that he had never felt before. Though Adam had no idea what to call it, he was being enveloped by the *numinosum* that flowed from the depths of his psyche.

It was as though his awareness had entered and become linked to each thing: every tree, rock, and bush he laid his eyes upon. As he gazed upon them, he became them and realized that the bigger part of himself contained everything that only appeared to be outside himself.

Bewildered, Adam continued to look about, pivoting on his feet, and turning about in a complete circle. All the woodland creatures shaking off the wetness of the night, nymphs, and fauns alike, paused in their routines and looked toward him, witnessing a glow that seemed to emanate from him. Though he could not see it himself, it enveloped him and everything around, including them.

It was then that all the creatures in this strange and otherworldly forest began welcoming him into their deep world of earth-wisdom—a world community with which nearly all but a handful of humans had lost touch over the millennia since they had separated themselves.

For the first time, he understood that this was his true self—the self hidden by his smaller ego-self. As himself, he was magic. He couldn't do anything as a separated self to make things happen except by being himself, his true self.

Body, Soul, and Divine Self or Spirit—Where Sun and Moon, Masculine and Feminine Become Whole

Craning his neck, he looked upward and saw the rising sun greeting his partner, the moon, who had been standing at his side but now greeted him with an embrace that partially occluded the brilliance of the groom's costume. The conjunction had begun.

He marveled at its beauty and the simplicity of its movement. The fear that had earlier consumed him had been replaced with quiet certainty.

As the sun climbed into the morning sky, more of it was absorbed by its companion until only a diamond-like sparkle remained and what had been two had become one. The marriage of opposites into this darkened sun was complete, and all who watched were absorbed into their union.

"The twins Apollo and Diana are together again," he said to himself.

With his feet planted in the earth, he became grounded in a trinity of earth, sun, and moon, becoming a part of their union and all coming together in his heart.

Casting out the folly of all reason, the final stage of the ancient melding of the salt of azoth, mercury, and sulfur that would form the philosophical stone in his heart and that would open him to the mystery of magic, the alchemical conjoining, was happening. It was like staring at a giant mandala or witches' circle hanging there in the sky and showing the way from the unconscious to the conscious and back again. As he had when he had stepped into the circle the magus had formed back at the house, he felt calm, centered, and assured, though he had a small amount of trepidation over what was next.

At that moment, a sacred and numinous holy and otherworldly presence consumed him and left him standing in awe.

He was now a soul transmuted into gold, and where he had once felt alone, he now felt connected to everything about him. What he had at one time felt were many he now realized that at the core had always been just one.

In a last effort to maintain its separateness, the ego-self desperately tried to reassert itself, but where once there had been a war waging within him of right or wrong, good or bad, love or hate, fear or peace, all seemed connected—not just connected, but with each originating in the other. He silently turned and faced the universal conjoining taking place both above and below, without and within. Everywhere he looked, he could see the magic working and creating.

Staring at the conjoined orb above, he was overwhelmed by the sense of a great spirit whose hand reached out to him and held him firm and steady between heaven and earth, the father and mother, his father and mother, who had come together, embracing him, and giving birth to yet another new beginning. Though the separated light from each orb had been diminished in their conjoining, a deeper, more nourishing, light was being revealed.

At this realization, a tunnel appeared before him, and he felt pulled toward it. As he stepped forward, the images of both mare and buck seemed to be drawn into him. He knew instinctively that this marked a new beginning being revealed, and he unhesitatingly walked into this long, undulating wormhole of a passage when a pulsating round aperture appeared at its far end, filled with light and beckoning.

Both fear and instinct worked on him, pushing him forward and holding him back. The walls began to close in upon him and squeeze him toward the light, though he tried to resist, but some part of him longed for the light at the end. It was so confusing!

As his body struggled with these two opposing forces, something just at the edge of awareness was working its way toward consciousness. While being forced toward the light, there was an "other-something" deep inside that was pushing its way to the surface of his awareness. For a moment, it felt almost malevolent in its intention, and it seemed that if he succumbed, it would irrevocably change his world. Did he want this change? Could he stop it if he didn't? Panicking, he again tried to resist the push, but something wanted to be born, and there was no turning it back.

Breaking through the opening at the end of the tunnel, he found himself once again on the rain-soaked path of a more familiar terrain. Gone was the endless tract of woodland that had heretofore defined the space of the conjoining. In its place was the park at the end of the street. A playful wisp of mist swirled and danced about his feet as though to welcome him back.

His reactive body and mind that before now were always distracting him by continually demanding his conscious attention seemed to dissolve into the infinite.

In a single breath taken as a gasp, a scream worked its way from gut to mouth and erupted into the early morning light. As the plaintive shout of a newly born soul came into being and slowly died out, all thought was transcended and a quiet beingness fell upon him.

He became acutely aware of everything: the gray-green leaves on the trees, the vibrant colors on others, their branches, the pleasant smell of the rain-soaked earth, the crisp lightning smell of the air, the skittering of creatures making way as he passed—everything. He walked slowly, and the leaves whose lives had been spent and had fallen during the night were ground into the earth, and he knew they would, in their death, create nourishment for the trees still waving their branches in the breeze.

Death had no power over him now, for he had become as small as the smallest leaf and in so doing had become grounded in everything around him. For a short while that had the feel of an eternity, a sense of gentle love, humility, virtue, and natural belonging filled every cell of his being.

Yet there was a wildness all about him that had always been there, entwined with the gentle souls of nature, and both had caught him up in their embrace. And in this blended reality he found peacefulness and belonging.

Love, the consumer of souls, had eaten him, and he had become it.

Looking out across the panorama of the city spread out before him, he could see a radiant rainbow arching across the entry into the bay. It was an apparition both material and immaterial, both lunar and solar in essence. He knew that it represented the way home. Anchored upon the earth at both ends, it represented the eternal mandala of the hidden whole.

During the long, dark night, he had found the mother, the Empress Astronomia her name, and had come home to the holy place of her magic and had found the source; she had been there all along. The quickening was complete.

Whatever had happened to him as the sun and moon came together in that early morning, he had survived the conjunction and was feeling more whole, more complete, than he had ever felt before. Even the world that had seemed so harsh after the loss of his family had, as if by magic, somehow become more stable and more inviting.

But he was still cautious, for there had been times during the night when he had thought the trials had passed only to be met with yet another.

At this thought, a loud flapping of some winged creature swooped down over his right shoulder, and inky black feathers brushed against his cheek and caused him to slightly recoil. Turning quickly to see what it was that threatened, there before him on the path he saw that a raven had lighted and appeared to be laughing while hopping all about. It was a silly-looking bird, a trickster of sorts, hopping awkwardly from one leg to the other while twisting in circles and screaming what for all the world sounded like "It is done, it is done!"

Surly this was Rubio, the fourth of the spirit guides the magus had told him would come. This was the one that completed the predicted quaternity and brought with it a symbol of achieved wholeness. The stone in his pocket seemed to grow warmer.

As he stared, this inky black trickster appeared to morph between a deep black and snow white. While behaving like a dervish, his feathered cloak blinked black and white like a beacon flashing on and off, on and off, over, and over, deepening the effect of the night upon Adam's soul.

The incongruity between this silly little show and what had taken place during the night was not lost on Adam, and despite himself he stood there laughing along with this last visitor the magus had told him would come. He knew then that the transformation through this dark night journey of the soul was complete.

Had it been real? Had the spirits he had encountered spoken to him, or was it all just his imagination? Whether they had been real or not, he thought there was a change in him.

Wiping the rain from his face and slicking back his rain-soaked hair, he was drenched but glowing with an inner warmth and sense of safety that he hadn't felt since his early childhood.

"Thank you all," whispered the young man to all the creatures and spirits above and below, bowing slightly. "I see the magic that's always been there, and I thank you deeply for opening my eyes to it." A slight breeze brushed his cheek in response.

Happily, he turned and walked briskly. But then, full of unrestrained energy, he began running back wildly toward town—a town that he was seeing so vividly and clearly for what seemed to be the first time. Soon he found himself standing before the entrance to the old magician's home, taking it in as he had never done before.

With a big sigh and growing excitement, he virtually hopped into the old man's apartment without even so much as a knock or a "by your leave." Dripping onto the foyer floor, he beamed into the room with a silly grin that literally lit up everything.

Sitting by the warming fire, the magus raised his cup in acknowledgment of the young man's successful return. Nodding his receipt of the acknowledgment, the boy shook off the water from his jacket, hung it on the hook and strode triumphantly into the kitchen, where he tested the warmth of the kettle on the stove by lightly touching its side, grabbed a cup at the sink, and poured himself something hot. There was always something brewing in this kitchen: freshly cut teas with rose hips, Ethiopian coffee beans ready for grinding, shaved chocolate, and even mulled wine. He never knew what he was going to get when he poured from the kettle. Taking a sip, he was delighted, for it was his favorite: strong coffee laced with a little cream and cinnamon. He then returned to the fire, whose dancing fairy denizens seemed to crackle a happy sound in honor of his return.

As he bent down, a chair moved itself beneath him, and he plopped into it, giving out a long and pleasant sigh. He noted that the most nourishing moments that he had with his mentor often occurred with a cup in hand. But it was more than what was in the cup because it was as though the cup offered spiritual nourishment to the healing of his soul. Over time it had taken on the aspect of a communion chalice symbolic of the union of their spirits.

With steaming mug in hand, the old man asked the boy, "All is well?" knowing full well that it was; otherwise, the boy wouldn't be there.

"It is," Adam said almost matter-of-factly.

"Then there is much work to do!" exclaimed the old wizard over the edge of the cup he was drinking from. He blew softly across its surface to cool it before taking another sip. He then put it down and rose to his feet. "Come; I have something to show you."

With a curious look toward the retreating wizard, the young man put down his cup and followed the old man out the door and onto the street. The old wizard motioned him toward a newly painted sign that had been affixed beside the door. Adam thought it odd that he hadn't noticed this new addition when he had entered just moments earlier. The younger man read it quietly and smiled.

"Yes, there *is* a lot to do," he agreed jovially.

As they climbed arm on shoulder back into the flat, anyone, had he or she been looking, could not have helped but notice the new sign affixed to the wall outside the door, which read in bright metallic gold,

HERMES AND ADAM, LLC
PURVEYORS OF QUALITY MAGIC

The green book, with odd hand-drawn illustrations.

CHAPTER 8

The Prima Materia: The Freed Spirit and Its Soul

Lose yourself completely. Return to the root of your own soul.

—Rumi

"*Hermes,*" *whispered* Adam. "His name is Hermes. How curious! How is it I never thought to ask?"

Hermes knew at that moment that once again, as he had predicted in the beginning of this relationship, the chemistry between him and Adam had worked its magic upon him and had changed his connection with reality and the world he had been living so comfortably in. His own transformation was also nearly complete. Intuitively, he knew what he must do.

As they entered the house once again, the magus turned to the young man and said, "I must ready myself to leave. This is your place now. Be open to it and it will meet your every need and entertain your every desire."

The space between them was filled by an ever-deepening silence as Adam wrestled with what his mentor had just shared. When his mind again whirled into action, he spoke quietly and with focus, carefully measuring every word.

"I don't understand. I thought you said that there was a lot for us to do," he uttered haltingly, with a bit of choking on the words at the possibility that the old man and he would not be working together anymore.

"Ah, you misunderstand. What you have been going through was just the beginning of your journey. It has been your process of atonement—not the guilt-ridden form offered in some religious sects, but your process of becoming 'at-one-ment' with all there is and your process of becoming whole.

"There are those who call themselves Buddhists who speak of a wisdom journey that brings forth awareness of the natural world. This is the journey both you and I have been on. This is a new day for both of us—a day when we both begin again.

"You now have much to give to the world and to those who venture upon your door. The mother has touched you, and you must pass it on. You are now freed to do that. And I now must move on to my next assignment. What I said is that there is much to do."

"But the sign out front has both our names."

"Also true, for you and I will always be linked, as I am with all my teachers and forebears. You now belong to all of them, and they to you. It is this connection that makes it possible to do this work. You now inherit all my teachers, including the spirit of the house, which is the alchemical still that will aid in all your future transformations."

"Alchemical still?" implored Adam.

"Remember when you were surrounded by the vase-like apparition as your body caught fire during your first dissolution?"

"Would be hard to forget," muttered Adam.

"That was the house acting as an alembic, or alchemical still, for your transformation."

"Ah yes, I remember it well. Scary as hell!"

Hermes smiled at that and went on with his explanation. "You are part of a family that stretches back many millennia. Honor each of them for every one of your days, for they will help you to regain your soul on those days when all seems lost.

"You and the house are charged with taking care of each other. It can be a bit cranky at times, but it will serve you well when you learn to listen to it. Stoke your own inner fire, and the fireplace that gave you a new beginning will continue to warm you throughout your days.

"I charge you as well with this goal for your life: may you always be a blessing to all whom you meet and know that to keep what you have become you need to also give it away. Keep giving of yourself and you will never truly be without. And as I have said so often before, cling to nothing, because that will obscure the magic and waste energy in its keeping.

"Lastly I leave you my special green book—a grimoire that outlines the Hermetic transformation that you have gone through and all its secrets. Now that you can see where the magic lies, the otherwise blank pages will become known to you. There is much obvious and hidden meaning throughout its pages that you will discover as you grow and experience. In it you will discover the hidden power of four that I alluded to some time ago and that you have personally experienced throughout your transformation. There are writings from the Kabbalist's *Tetragrammaton* and from Pythagoras' *Tetractys*, the four seasons and the four classical elements, all with their transcendent meaning. In here you will also find a version of the four labors of Psyche, in whose dream you are living, with emphasis on the fourth, where one needs to give up the body and all its illusions to join the body with spirit to complete oneself and see the magic.

"It also contains thirteen books with hidden layers of meaning that will become more visible as you grow and brighten in your skill, which will only happen as you pass on its wisdom to others. Within these books lie several logia that will, like so many koan, challenge your understanding and growth. But understand you must, because in your struggle with them you will discover the unifying principles of the universe and the riotous dynamism in which it expresses itself."

"Can I still see you from time to time?" queried the young man, who had grown most fond of the old wizard.

"Of course! You and I live within the nontemporal eternity of the here and now, where past and present come together, and in that space we can always meet. You now know who you are, and by this you know who I am, because you are me, and I am you, and we are both whole. As one of my mentors once wrote, 'Thou art that.' You now know that our souls are old friends that have known one another across the ages."

"I'm also everyone I meet, so I guess in that case I'll always be working with myself and with you."

The old sage smiled and once again stated, "I think he has got it! Now, one last thing before I go," he offered as a small valise appeared in one hand while a staff bearing a snake coiled about its shaft materialized in the other. "The challenges in your life will not disappear, but you now have a new way in which to meet them. This is not the end of your training but the beginning. There may also be times when what you have gained will seem to fade but focus and intention will keep them strong in the long run, and that intentionality will become second nature the more you practice it.

"You now know of the light and must pass it on in every moment and in every circumstance, for this light is what makes space for the creation of something bigger than yourself. Know that even in your darkest times there is light shining within. It will always be there, and you need but look for it. You are now one of the knowers. You have discovered that the degree to which you, as a knower, go beyond yourself—that is, beyond your pride and madness, self-will, and ego-centered cunning to function out of spirit and love—is the degree to which you can be magic and function in a magical way."

At this Adam moved closer and gave his mentor a great and somewhat lingering hug, trying to commit to memory the scent of both the mentor and the house as he did so. But he would not soon forget his old teacher's aroma of cherry pipe tobacco, coffee, and old parchment—a mix that would linger for many years in the old house and remind him of this magical time with his teacher.

"See you later!" Adam whispered as his eyes smarted, and he choked back the tears.

"Of course!" cried the wizard with a broad smile, and he turned to go, disappearing before reaching the door.

Somewhat bewildered and scratching his head, Adam looked around with whole new eyes at what just a moment ago had been the abode of his mentor. He had very little knowledge of what secrets the house held but was pretty sure that with time he'd figure out how to communicate with it. Perhaps something about this was in the green book.

Resting on the table was the emerald-green tablet that the old wizard had given him, and he reached for it and opened to the first page, which had once been blank but now mysteriously began with a cryptic story written with great care upon its vellum pages, through a scribe's well-trained hand, inked with a feathered quill and employing an odd mix of old and new expressions. Clearly it had been penned in the hand of the departed wizard.

Curious, he thumbed through the book, noting that there were still several blank pages, but these were now interspersed among other pages written in several different hands and many languages. There were ancient Arabic, Aramaic, Sanskrit, Maya, Chinese, Hindi, Egyptian, Greek, French, Hebrew, German, Slavic, Sioux, Ogham, and medieval and modern English commentaries and formulae with odd hand-drawn illustrations. It was a virtual compendium and praxis of, meaning the path toward, the world's magic. In this book were the answers to how to rid the mind of the duality of thinking that keeps the psyche separated and unable to be magic.

And sure enough, as Hermes had said, there were several logia that, like some of the mage's other quotes, made little sense, such as one stating that you must "come into being as you pass away." He'd have to ponder that one later.

Oddly enough, though he knew not every language, the longer he stared upon the writings, the more readable they became. However, the drawings seemed more to be metaphors than actual depictions of reality and would no doubt take him longer to decipher, given his lack of knowledge of the customs and historical contexts of their authors.

Returning to the first page, he scanned the words written by the wizard, and as he read them, it appeared to be a tale of the old man's journey as he first set out on his own path. Adam chuckled to himself, for he was pretty sure that this was the old man's final lesson to him as he began his own journey. He also noticed that there was a part in the old man's story that curiously reflected his own experience of transformation.

MCCCLXX

On my walk today, I met an old man sitting cross-legged in his stall and stirring with his pot-styke some concoction in an iron vessle.

"What ho?" I inquired, but he did not answer and continued to stere the vessle. "Can I see what is in your pot?" I asked as he continued to stir.

Not waiting for an answere, I leaned forward to gain a glimpse of what was stirring, and all went black. Images indiscriminate whirled and whorled about, taking and losing form as I tried to focus upon them. All moved like thickened liquid and climbed the sides of the pot, only to be pulled back into its muck.

"What is this place so darke and of undefined form?" I moaned as I was being drawn into its depths.

It was then that the old man spake, and my eares inclined. "It is of thou, the hidden thou, thou of many generations and many worelds."

"Why do you speak in riddles, old man?" I gasped.

"Because your kind cannot understand when confronted directly with the truth," he blurted bluntly. "You seek an answere to a questen you have not fully understood. Because of this, its answere will sit in seacret at your core until you are ready to open the door with its locks twelve.

"Meanwhile, the seacret lies within the chaos darke. Understand your questen and the keye that will open all the lok will reveal itself to you, and of the chaos you will know, and the darknes will be hiden no more."

"Tell me, alchemist, about this keye of which you speak," I demanded gently.

"Learn the true seacret invisible of the three and the two that are one and dispel the myth of the priests who know not any seacrets save their own making, and the keye will be revealed. It is only in the one conjoined body that the seacrets reveal." The old man very deliberately kept stirring the pot.

"But once I have it, how will I know to which lok it fits, for it cannot fit all of them, can it?"

"There is but one lock for all. But its knowing maistery can only appear through the vision clere of every lok. It is for you to look truly, and it will reveal. You cannot distill what is needed while you live in the above ground. You must enter downe into the chaos of the darknes to do that.

"The answere is not to be found in the nonsense of your wakened state, for it only comes in the darke furnace heate of the chaos to be then congealed and carried unto the light.

"The answere is not obtained by sword or will of minde but by grace. You must dissolve the hardness of the waking minde through the softness of the darknes; only then will the questen become clere enough for you to see the keye

and the lock it opens. Only then can you pass through the door and find the stone of eternity promised by the divine philosophers."

My minde began to swim like the stirring liquid of his pot, and I swam desperate for its surface. Breaking free of his spell, I stood wetted and dripping afore him, but before I could yet speak again, he smiled and dissolved in front of me, and I awoke.

Had I been in sleepe? I had not been in my bedde, for I was sure that I had been walking an old and familiar path, and yet my eyes seemed opened clere to something new, and I could see then that I needed to look within and enter this sacred space of the chaos darke with the questen "What is in there that is for me to find?" For it was there that the magic of my own hidden will resides as a darknes and a light that feeds the upper psyche, causing a new seeing to appear.

Da gloriam Deo,
Hermes

Upon finishing the story written long ago by his mentor, he again smiled to himself and remarked to no one in particular, "You are right, old friend, and in the darkness, I will remember where the light can always be found." As he slowly closed the book, he reflected fondly upon how his life had changed so much since standing before the door of this house not so many days ago and wondering what was yet to come.

EPILOGUE

Opus continuum

We men and women are all in the same boat, upon a stormy sea. We owe to each other a terrible and tragic loyalty.

—G. K. Chesterton

Adam settled into his new house but continued to go to school and eventually graduated with a degree in history with an emphasis on mythology. During this time, he finally mustered up the courage to talk to the barista at his favorite coffee shop and asked her out. She, it turned out, was completing her master's in ecological science and sustainability. Over time their friendship blossomed and became closer and more serious. It was his powerful humility that drew her to him and him to her, with each more interested in the welfare of the other, with each bearing witness to the other, and with each sharing the other's soul. Together they founded a nonprofit group known as the Magic of Caring Project, which supported many successful endeavors both locally and internationally.

Because she tended to be a planner and organizer by nature, and Adam the actualizer of the plan, they made a very successful team.

Sarah turned out to be a natural at being present to the magic and in this way became yet another teacher for Adam. She, like her ancient feminine forebears, expanded the art of soul transmutation and magic.

Many seasons flitted by as they were married for some sixty-five years and raised four children in the old house, which never seemed to get old, high in the city above the bay.

The children laughed and played in the marvelous old place with its magic and mystery, which provided hours of entertainment, but even after a lifetime the house remained a mystery to Adam. Many a story was told by their daddy of his old mentor, which kept the children mesmerized for years.

Though all four children followed their own spirit guides and gave much of themselves to the world they found themselves in, one of the girls, Ginny, followed in her dad's footsteps, found the magic, and traveled with her mother throughout the world, sharing and helping others to awaken to their true nature.

During this time, Hermes had been very busy traveling between time streams. But shortly after their marriage, Adam and Sarah ran into him during a visit to the Glastonbury Tor, a place it is said is a gateway to many historical streams that come together. When they were looking out at the rolling landscape beyond the tor, Hermes walked out of an early morning mist that had formed about the top of the hill and greeted the couple.

They also ran into each other at various other sacred places over the years and shared that they were both continuing the work that his mentor had introduced him to and through the alchemical process had nourished many and had awakened to the magic several other young men and women who had come to their door. The stories and the revelations they provided were added to the stories that filled some of the blank pages in the green book. Ah, but Hermes's sojourns through the Everwhen is a story for another time.

Adam and Sarah continue to live in the old Victorian and for many years have regaled their grandchildren as well as their grandchildren's children with the stories of the magic of their lives.

ACKNOWLEDGMENTS

And above all, watch with glittering eyes the whole world around you because the greatest secrets are always hidden in the most unlikely places. Those who don't believe in magic will never find it.

—Roald Dahl, *The Minpins* (1991)

Because no one person has the level of awareness to envision all that is magical in the world, I want to acknowledge those whose ideas informed certain aspects of this story. The knowledge of the magical realm and how to access it is an ancient knowledge that has come down through the words of many "wizards," some of whom I recognize here. All have expressed a special understanding of the world of spirit and magic that is woven into the fabric of our world.

I thank Carl G. Jung for the term "Shadow Self" and its description. Elias Ashmole, who wrote the *Theatrum Chemicum Britannicum* (1652), provided the concept of the "Chaos Darke," which I then translated into the concept of the unconscious mind. The idea of integrating the shadow, or animal, self also shows up in Hermes's instruction to Adam "Here you need to eat the lion rather than to allow him to eat you." This is a paraphrase from the Gospel of Thomas, Logion 7.

Use of the idea that dreams come to us in the service of our health

141

and well-being came from the books on dream interpretation written by Jeremy Taylor.

The idea that death can be a vitality in that it can organize the way in which one can live one's life is an idea I learned when attending a lecture by the philosopher Dr. Peter Koestenbaum back in the early to mid-1970s at a local university.

The concept of redirecting the energy you use in attending to your dreams and how energy in maintaining one's self-importance drains that energy is an approach discussed in Carlos Castaneda's book *The Art of Dreaming* (Harper Collins, 1993).

It was also through Castaneda's book *A Separate Reality* (Simon and Schuster, 1971) that I first became entranced with the idea of living life as though death were a constant companion hovering over my shoulder, which was also echoed by the philosophy of Peter Koestenbaum, mentioned above.

In this book Castaneda also brought up through the character of the shaman Don Juan the idea of "feeling" the world in its entirety, which Hermes first broaches with Adam early in their dialogue. This also reflects an experience that I had one crazy evening after a long meditation at a Zen retreat in the mountains overlooking the Santa Clara Valley. Castaneda's concept of silent knowing that shows up in chapter 6 (i.e., a knowing that doesn't engage the cognitive system) was also a concept discussed through the character of Don Juan.

The placebo effect upon the body–mind connection used by many shamans throughout the world was in part responsive to an article by Fabrizio Benedetti published by the Oxford University Press in November 2014.

The reference to "a glass darkly" comes from Paul in Corinthians 13:12 in the Christian Bible. The phrase "Believe in Allah but tie up your Camel" is attributed to Muhammad in the book, *Sunan al-Tirmidhī*, one of the six books from the hadith collection (CE 864/5).

The saying "say a prayer but move your feet" is a phrase used in South Africa but also the favorite saying of the recently deceased John Lewis, the American politician and civil rights activist.

The phrase "He looked this way and that and saw no one" has been attributed to Moses (Exodus 2:12).

The discussion about good and bad was partially derived from Carl Jung's thoughts about the subject in his book *Psychology and Alchemy* (1968, Bollingen Foundation).

Jung's musings about the reality of magic were taken from several of his books, including *The Red Book* and the translations by Sanford Drob in his book *Reading the Red Book* (2012, Spring Journal), and Jung's book *Memories, Dreams, Reflections* (1969, Vintage Books) informed some of the sections on the laws of magic.

The alchemical transformation process outlined for Adam was loosely fashioned from the process depicted in the alchemical manuscript *Splendor Solis,* Harley MS 3469 (modern edition by M. Moleiro, from the 1582 original).

In chapter 4 Hermes declares, *"solve et coagula"* (to dissolve and coagulate, or to separate and then join). It is a quote from medieval alchemical texts.

The quote at the beginning of this work comes from George Ripley, a fifteenth-century English alchemist, and was found in Elias Ashmole's book *Theatrum Chemicum Britannicum,* page 398 (1652). This also inspired the figure 1 drawing.

The snake spirit image, as presented by Hermes in the story, is an amalgam of the ideas presented by Joseph Campbell from his book *The Inner Reaches of Outer Space* (Harper Perennial, 1986). The power of the kundalini that has transforming qualities and whose coiled figure is carved above Hermes's fireplace is as old as the ninth-to-tenth-century BCE Upanishads.

The ideas of soul and "core self," and the limiting of children's destiny by the grown-up world are from my own experience of working with children for more than thirty years and are roughly presented and altered to fit this story from *The Soul's Code* by James Hillman (Random House, 1996). The ideas regarding the trinity of body, soul, and spirit were modeled after the writings of Thomas Moore, who wrote *The Care of the Soul* (Harper Collins, 1992).

While being reconstituted from the ashes, Adam's soul was purified through music. This notion comes from an idea offered by Pythagoras (580–500 BCE). He and some of his followers believed that there was an unheard melody in the universe that had a powerful influence on the physical world.

Also, while being a nothing after being burned to ash, Adam recalls a quote from a Mr. Descartes, which refers to the philosopher René Descartes, who was quoted as saying, "I think therefor I am." He made this statement basically because he reasoned that his existence was needed for him to have thoughts; therefore, his thinking proved his existence.

The discussion on forgiveness, resentment, and reconciliation was in part from the story of St. Benedict, an early sixth-century Christian monk, from the writings of Pope Gregory I, and from my own work with abused children.

The "softening of the ego" is an ancient wisdom from Lao Tzu and the sixth-century BCE Tao Te Ching.

The green book that sat beside the chair of Hermes and was passed onto Adam is a loose reference to the emerald tablet (a.k.a. Tabula Smaragdina) attributed to the ancient magus Hermes Trismegistus.

Hermes was (is?) an ancient Greek semi deity spoken of by Cicero, the statesman and scholar of ancient Rome. The Hermetic literature (Corpus Hermeticum), or wisdom texts, many of the insights of which he was the assumed author, showed Hermes to be a teacher of disciples in the arts of the divine, cosmic, alchemical, astrological, and natural environments.

The sage Hermes as he appears in this story exhibits some of the aspects written down by ancient Arabic and Egyptian scholars but also represents an amalgam of several wisdom keepers whom I have had the pleasure of learning from over the years.

The concepts of the "Beginner's Mind" and being present and mindful were fashioned from the teachings of Shunryū Suzuki. The "door to perception" idea was adapted from William Blake's book of eighteenth-century poems, *The Marriage of Heaven and Hell.*

Sprinkled throughout the story are also the heart and soul of such luminaries as Buddha, Jewish mystics, Muhammad, and Jesus of Nazareth. Their path was the path of magic.

The idea that we are living within an illusion of reality was partially constructed from my own experiences, the teachings in *A Course in Miracles*, and from several other sources, including the writings of modern quantum physicists.

The concept of space and time being two sides of the same coin can be surmised from Albert Einstein's theories of relativity.

The phrase "Thou art that," spoken by Hermes in chapter 8, is a translation of "tat tvam asi," from the Hindu scriptures the Upanishads.

The figure of speech "It is a poor sense of time that only moves forward" is pulled from Lewis Carroll's book *Alice in Wonderland*, where can be found the original phrase "It's a poor memory that only works backwards."

The symbol underlying the Introduction, chapter headings, and the Acknowledgment section, has multifold meaning. Traditionally this is the symbol of the philosopher's stone, which in this story represents the metamorphosis of the psyche. It is surrounded by the four elements: from the top and moving clockwise, these are fire, water, earth, and air. Each takes the stage at various moments throughout the story. These elements create a square around the circle, representing the basic Jungian archetype of wholeness—what is needed to express the magic within the story.

The term "quaternity" is a Latin word meaning "four of something." Its use as a symbol for wholeness within the psyche was used by Carl Jung, who thought of the number four as being an archetype that points to the process of becoming whole in the human psyche. It is the process of the unity of psyche's opposing aspects.

The centering prayer that Hermes teaches Adam comes from a contemplative tradition going back to the Middle Ages. The current form of the prayer, using Psalm 46:10 from the Hebrew scriptures, was popularized for our times by Thomas Merton, the American Trappist monk.

The invocation by Adam during the rainstorm when all seemed lost follows the beliefs and language style of the tradition of the Jewish mystics, the Kabbalah (קַבָּלָה), where one entreats to do and undo something following a prescribed pattern of words considered to have magical power. This is not unusual, for many traditions have shown the power of language to alter one's reality.

The names of the mother (e.g., Aerial, Gabriela, Jophiela, and Uriela) are feminine forms of archangels found in the Abrahamic religions but are also similar to figures from other religious traditions (e.g., Zoroastrianism) and were known as "immortal holiness." Their spellings have been slightly altered.

This story of Adam's transformation comes from the unconscious personal and collective archetypes that have revealed themselves to me over a lifetime of working with the magic of Psyche's dreams and the very real inner dragons of so many, as well as my own.

The word "numinous" shows up throughout the story and becomes especially evident in chapter 7 with the concept of the numinosum, or spirit, an experience of the mystical that can present a person with a hint of something greater than what the ego is conscious of. It is often experienced as a oneness with all things. It comes from the philosophical work of the German Lutheran theologian and philosopher Rudolph Otto.

Near the end of the story, Hermes talks about the "wisdom journey" that Adam has been on. The concept of wisdom in this story incorporates the idea of the Buddhist Pāramitā, or the culmination of certain virtues (e.g., the purification of karma and the helping of one to live an unobstructed life—a concept integral to the experience of magic).

Also, near the end of the story Adam comes across the logia, or aphorism, "Come into being as you pass away." This is logion 42 from the Gospel of Thomas found in the Nag Hamadi documents of the life of Jesus that did not make it into the New Testament.

I also want to acknowledge my children and grandchildren, each of whom has shown me the magic that exists in everything around and within me. They are proof positive of the magic of love.

All these wizards have shown the courage to just be themselves, no matter how different that looked to the rest of the world.

ABOUT THE AUTHOR

R. J. Cole is a retired educational psychologist who worked with adjudicated youth in juvenile detention centers and children's shelters throughout California, and with children diagnosed with severe emotional disturbance and autism, and their families.

In Santa Clara County, California, during the 1980s through to the early 2000s, Cole established several day treatment classrooms on regular-education school campuses using the regular classroom and public-school campus environment as part of the children's therapy with the goal of shifting their response to the reality of the school and social experience. This bucked the trend of the day, where emotionally disturbed students were taught in centers away from their normal peers. It was during this time that Cole started delving into the magical world of dreams and using students' dreams as both a diagnostic and therapeutic tool to help enter the children's realities, often with great success.

Cole has written four books on the theme of dreams and their meanings and application plus several academic manuals on affective education, behavior management, and meditation.

Cole currently lives in California with his wife, Fran, and continues to share and read the dreams of his family members and of the many thousands across the world who have sent him their dreams through his blogs and websites.

Printed in the United States
by Baker & Taylor Publisher Services